Matthias

THE GHOST OF SALVATION POINT

Jodi Auborn

To my dad, who loved lighthouses and the sea.

Lou Auborn
1950 - 2014

Prologue

Salvation Point, Maine
February 1913

*A*s the wind whistled past the lantern room windows, Matthias knew that he had never seen such a blizzard in the twenty-five years that he had worked at the lighthouse. The waves, far below, devoured the cliffs and threw their spray as high as the tower itself, while the freezing rain soon changed to snow. The thick flakes fell so heavy that Matthias couldn't even see the railing outside. He was thankful for the safety of the lighthouse, and glad that he wasn't at sea.

But it wasn't always that way.

He stared out at the falling snow and remembered another storm, the summer thunderstorm that had changed his life and family forever. Though the years had passed, it felt like it had all happened yesterday. He was a young man then...

The deck bucked and heaved under his boots as he fought to keep the fishing schooner on course. He could see the lighthouse beam as it cut through the driving sea spray, when…CRACK! The foremast snapped like a twig and crashed to the deck, drowning out his father's cries for help, as he lay tangled in the fallen rigging. Matthias left the wheel and stumbled across the deck as the waves threw the helpless boat onto the rocks. She's sinking fast, *he thought.* I don't have much time. *He reached out for his father, only to see him disappear beneath the waves…*

Four months later, the old horse's hooves clopped down the dirt road, pulling the wagon that carried him off to the place where he'd spend the rest of his life. His mother sat beside him as birds chirped in the deep spruce forest and gentle waves lapped the rocks beside the bay. He should've been happy with this chance to make a new start, but he just stared straight ahead as his mother chattered on with her last-minute advice.

"…You know that I'm going to worry about you, living out here all by yourself. You're twenty years old, Matthias, and you're not getting any younger. It's time that you find a nice girl, and settle down. Plenty of other light keepers have a wife and children to help with the chores. And perhaps it might help you move on from…you know."

"Oh, Mama!" Matthias stopped the wagon and gestured at the red-roofed cottage and white lighthouse at the end of the road. "You have to understand. I won't have time for that sort of thing. This is going to be my life, now. The boat is destroyed, and my father is dead. I can't allow those cliffs to claim any more lives."

His mother reached over and patted his big rough hand, tears glistening in her eyes. "That accident on that boat was not your fault, son. Nobody blames you for what happened…"

The memory faded as he pulled his coat tighter around his thin body, and looked at his pocket watch. It was almost time to trim the wicks. In another hour, he'd have to wind the clockwork mechanism so the huge Fresnel lens would continue to rotate. It was a familiar routine, the same chores that he had done every night since he became the only keeper of the Salvation Point lighthouse.

The job didn't pay much, but he didn't ask for much, either. Back in the cottage he had books to read, his calico cat for company, and even his old upright piano in the parlor. His mother had taught him to play it as a young boy, and he was glad that there was music to fill the lonely cottage. He had all that he needed...

CRASH!

Matthias spun around as glass exploded into the room and something whizzed past his head, just missing the fragile glass lens. He examined the lens for damage – thankfully, none – and looked across the room at a piece of heavy driftwood lying on the floor. It must've come from the forest across the bay, thrown high by a wave, but that didn't matter. One of the windowpanes was broken, and had to be repaired at once! He knew that it was dangerous to go out in the storm, but he couldn't allow the lamp to burn out on a night like this! The sailors depended on him and his light to make it home safe.

The snow stung his face as he stepped out onto the gallery, the balcony outside the lantern room where he was going to inspect the broken window. He bent low into the wind, clamping his hat down on his head with one hand and gripping the icy railing with the other. Thick ice coated the whole lighthouse top, some hidden under the drifting snow.

Matthias gasped as a gust of wind knocked him off his feet. He didn't have a chance against the wind and ice as he slipped underneath the railing, flailing for a grip on something – anything – to keep him from falling fifty feet to the rocks below. His hands closed around an iron railing post, so heavy with ice that he knew he couldn't hang on for long. He looked down, even though he couldn't see the rocks through the swirling snow, the jagged granite that could take his life.

With all his strength, Matthias swung his leg back up and onto the ledge, but it was too icy to get a foothold on the slippery stone. He could feel the ice melting under his numb hands as he hung from the lighthouse top, fighting the wind that tried to tear him away. He remembered other times when he had nearly fallen, but had always been able to climb back to safety.

This time it was different.

Nobody heard his scream as the cold iron slipped from his hands.

CHAPTER I

Salvation Point

June 2013

*W*elcome to Salvation Point, Maine, population 550.

"We're finally here!" I cried as we passed the sign heading into town. We were a long way from our apartment in New York City, but I was glad that we made it here at last.

Back in May – just before my birthday - my dad found out that he had inherited a house from his Uncle Zack. But it wasn't just *any* house. Uncle Zack was a hermit who had lived in an old lighthouse keeper's house, right next to the ocean. He had owned a *real* lighthouse…and we were going to live there *all* summer!

As we drove into town, I thought about the day when my sister and I got home from school, and Dad told us that we had a new place to live…

"I remember visiting Uncle Zack at the cottage when I was growing up," Dad had told us. "The cottage is small, and very old, but it has three bedrooms. Two of them are upstairs in the attic."

"Dad?" I asked. "Maybe you and Mom can quit your jobs and become lighthouse keepers, and we could move there for *good!*"

"We don't have to take care of the lighthouse," Dad said. "Even though it's on our property, it's maintained by the Coast Guard. And it's all been automated. That means that it has modern equipment, and the light will come on by itself. A person from the Coast Guard just has to come and check it sometimes, to make sure that it's working right."

"Thank goodness for that," my sister, Alondra, grumbled. "Now, tell me: *how* long are we going to be stuck there?"

Alondra was fifteen, and she was the most *boring* person I knew. All she liked to do was hang out in stores with her friends, and try on *shoes* and *clothes*. We had nothing in common. And we didn't get along very well, either.

Alondra *hated* the whole idea of moving. Mom was nervous about leaving the city. But *me – I* couldn't wait to see the little town where Dad had grown up. He gave me a tourist guide-book so I could learn about Maine, but *Dad* wasn't a tourist. He had lived in Salvation Point his whole life, and worked at a shop where they repaired and built wooden boats. In the summer, he had been a sailing instructor at a camp for kids. Dad loved boats and the ocean, but when he married Mom, she had refused to leave the big city. Dad moved there and became an architect, but he always talked about moving back to Salvation Point someday.

Dad bought a car the week before we left. "There are no taxis or subways where we're going," he had said, smiling.

The day after fourth grade let out for the summer, we packed up the car and piled in for our long trip north to Maine. Alondra listened to her music and ignored Dad, who had spent the whole trip telling stories about his life growing up here.

After we passed the Salvation Point sign, I leaned forward and tapped Mom's shoulder. "Hey, Mom. Now that we're moving here, can we get a dog? I want a Newfoundland."

Mom frowned. "Dylan, we've already been through this. We'll only be here for the summer, and you know that we can't have pets at our apartment. Now, sit down and put your seatbelt back on. And be careful of my canvasses."

I sighed. I knew she'd say that. I stared out the window and moved my feet away from the pile of Mom's painting canvasses. She had stacked them behind Dad's seat before we left that morning.

My mom was an artist. I guess she was sort of famous. Her paintings were for sale at the *fanciest* art galleries all over the city, and only rich people could afford to buy them. But they did, and Mom became more famous every year.

"I must admit that this *is* a pretty town, Roger," Mom was telling Dad as we passed some big old houses. Most had flower gardens in the front yard, and shady porches with American flags that snapped in the breeze. Some kids my age rode their bikes down the sidewalk, goofing off and calling to each other.

Mom smiled at them. "I hope that you'll make an effort to make some friends this summer, Dylan," she said. "You're so *quiet* and *introverted*, like your father. It's not healthy."

Dad frowned at her. "Leave the boy alone, Rorianne. He's fine the way he is."

"Don't you get stern with *me*, Roger," Mom snapped. "You know that I'm only trying to help him."

I put my head down and smiled as Mom sulked. She was always telling Dad that she worried about me, or that I was "exasperating" her. She seemed to like that word: "exasperating." I guess I made her feel that way a lot. But I could always depend on Dad to keep Mom from nagging me too much. Dad was usually on my side.

At the edge of town, we went by a pizza parlor across the road from an old graveyard. Alondra shivered. "A *cemetery?* That's *not* what I want to look at while I'm eating pizza."

"That pizza place is called Pies on the Point. I can't believe that it's still here!" Dad said. He sounded as excited as a kid. "I hope the same family runs it. They made the best pizza that you'll ever eat."

"Then can we get some? I'm *hungry!*" I whined.

"Some other time; we'll be at the cottage in five minutes. Now, look over there, Dylan; that's the harbor. You and I are going to spend a lot of time there this summer."

Dad slowed down so I could get a good look at the harbor. All kinds of boats lined both sides of a long wooden dock, where two seagulls were fighting over a dead fish. Colorful buoys hung from some old gray buildings by the dock, and big powerboats floated at their moorings further out in the water. They weren't like the fancy yachts at the marina back home. These were long and low, with skinny smokestacks and covered wheelhouses with windows on three sides. They looked like they were made for work.

"What kind of boats are those?" I asked, pointing out the window.

"Those are lobster boats," Dad said. "I used to work on one when I was in high school…"

"Not another story!" Alondra groaned, as Dad started talking about his time working on the boat.

I looked behind us at *Thunder*, the little sailboat that Dad was towing. *Thunder* was mine. Dad had to hire a truck to haul his sailboat here, since it's bigger. His was docked at the harbor already.

After we passed the harbor, Dad turned onto a dirt road that ran along the edge of the bay. The breeze rustled the bushes alongside the road. They were covered with big pink flowers that Dad said were wild roses.

The other side of the road was all woods - nothing but dark green woods without any more houses in sight. The sun was starting to set behind the trees, casting dark shadows across the road and leaving a pale light glowing over the water.

"Look at all those trees!" I said, pointing at the woods. "They look like Christmas trees. Is that a big park?"

"Close. That's a nature preserve. And those aren't Christmas trees; they're spruces and firs. There are hiking trails all through those woods," Dad said.

"And I bet there's bears, too," Alondra muttered.

Dad shook his head. "Maybe not bears, but I'm sure there are coyotes...and *a lot* of deer and raccoons. Maybe even some moose. That side of the point is just woods, until you reach the lighthouse."

We passed a bald-headed man in a long, flapping coat, who prowled at the edge of the trees as if he didn't want anybody to catch him. He carried a big fancy-looking metal detector, and a long rolled-up paper under his arm. He looked up and stared as we went by, scratching the little beard on his chin. Dad waved, but the man just spit on the ground and watched as we continued down the road.

"Well, he doesn't look very nice, does he?" Mom said. "I don't like the way that he's just watching us." She shuddered and looked back at the town across the bay, hidden in the dark trees. "Roger, this place is *so* remote."

"Well, that's the really *great* thing!" Dad said with a smile. "Even though we have no close neighbors, we're only a mile from town. And tourists always stop here to take pictures of the lighthouse. We'll get plenty of company."

"Our nearest neighbor is a mile away? Roger, you *never* told me *that!*"

Dad just looked at her as he turned off the air conditioning and rolled down the windows. The wind smelled nice, like mud and wet rocks and warm, salty air.

I took a deep breath. "Smell that?" Dad said, smiling again. "That's the smell of low tide. We're home."

Up ahead, I spotted a house with a red roof. It looked like nobody had painted the house in a long time, but I didn't care about that. I was more interested in the lighthouse in the backyard. A person was walking around by the railing at the top. I couldn't wait to climb up there, too!

We left the woods behind us as Dad drove into a wide-open field surrounded by the ocean. "Well, here it is," he said, parking in front of the shabby-looking old house. "The Salvation Point Light Station."

CHAPTER 2

The Cottage

I was kind of disappointed when I looked at where we'd be spending the summer. I thought that we'd live in the little building attached to the lighthouse, not in this ordinary-looking house at the end of the driveway. Chips of peeling white paint clung to the old wooden siding. Dirty shades were pulled down over the windows, so we couldn't see inside. A broken plastic chair sat on the porch, as a piece of torn screen flapped in the breeze and a bamboo wind chime swayed from a low rafter.

Dad looked at the house and smiled. "I still can't believe that this is all ours!"

"Neither can I," Alondra grumbled. "What a dump. It's probably haunted."

Dad looked thoughtful. "You know, you could be right. This place has what you might call a...*reputation*. People have seen some scary stuff out here over the years. Strange lights, unexplained noises..."

"Roger, stop that! Don't frighten the children with such nonsense!"

"I'm not a *child*, Mom!" Alondra snapped.

"And *I* want to hear about the scary stuff," I said.

Mom sighed. "There is no *scary stuff*, Dylan. This is just a neglected old house that needs some paint, and cleaning up."

"Well, *I* like it."

Alondra sneered at me. "*You* would. You're just as weird as Uncle Zack."

"*Alondra!*" Mom said. "Don't tell your brother that! And your uncle wasn't weird, he was...eccentric."

"Yeah, just like Dylan," Alondra muttered. "Look, I still don't understand *why* we all had to move out here to the *country.*"

Dad sighed. "We're not in the *country*, Alondra. It's a small *town.*"

"Where? *I* didn't see any *town.*" She took her cell phone out of her purse. "I'm calling Julie."

Dad grinned. "You can't call *any* of your friends. There's no cell service here."

"You're kidding me!" Alondra wailed. "What kind of a place *is* this? I want you to take me home *right now!* If you don't, I'll walk. I don't care how long it takes!"

"Well, then you would have an awfully...long...walk. We're not far from the Canadian border." Dad was starting to lose his temper. "Fact is, we're about as down east as we can get."

"And what's *that* supposed to mean?"

"It *means*, that I'm not driving you all the way back to New York City! You're spending the summer here, and you're going to appreciate it. You know, a lot of people dream about owning a place like this."

Alondra tossed her hair over her shoulder. "Then they can *have* it!"

"Listen, young lady! It's going to be a long summer for you, if you've already made up your mind to hate it here. You need to accept the fact that we're not leaving until the end of August. And it will be good for you to get out of the city for a while. I want you and your brother to experience a simple, old-fashioned summer like the ones I had when I was a kid. Maybe you'll even learn something."

Alondra rolled her eyes. "It's *simple*, alright. Dad, this place is totally *dead*. There's *nobody* here!"

"That will change once the tourists and other summer people arrive. It gets really busy around here, then. The traffic is a nightmare. You should enjoy this while it lasts."

Alondra glared at Dad and muttered something as she grabbed her luggage and yanked it out of the car, slamming the door behind her.

I could hear the waves washing up on the rocks as I climbed out of the car and stretched. I had spent the whole trip squashed between two duffel bags and Mom's canvasses, smelling Alondra's perfume and my own sweat.

As we gathered up our bags, seagulls screamed as they flew over our heads and picked at things on the rocks by the lighthouse. The person I had seen up at the railing was gone.

"Dad? I thought I saw someone at the top of the lighthouse. But they're not there, now."

Dad shook his head. "It's impossible for anyone to be up there, Dylan. You could've seen a cloud formation, or a bird... just about anything. The lighthouse door is locked, and only myself and the Coast Guard have keys."

"It wasn't a *bird*," I grumbled. Alondra smirked at me and followed Mom and Dad as they headed for the house.

I looked up at the empty lighthouse top again, and then over at the harbor across the bay. I watched as a rusty lobster boat pulled up to the dock, and then hurried to catch up with everyone else.

We walked over some cracked stepping-stones through weeds that came up to my waist, and I thought I heard a... *piano* playing somewhere. It was really soft, as if the sound was just floating by on the wind.

"Listen, can you hear that?" Alondra asked.

We all stopped. "That piece is by Bach, I believe," Mom said. "Where in earth is it *coming* from?"

"It could be from town," Dad said. "The sound carries across the water."

"It sounds too close to be coming from *town*, Roger," Mom said.

The piano music grew louder and louder as we stepped up on the porch and Dad unlocked the door. The floorboards shook as the music pounded all around us.

I grabbed Dad's shirt and he hugged me against himself, both of us staring into the overgrown yard. Dad's suntanned face had turned white under his beard. Alondra hid her face in her hands and moaned. Mom grabbed Dad's arm and whipped her head all around, like she was searching for the invisible piano player. "IT'S JUST A RADIO PLAYING SOMEWHERE; IT *MUST* BE A RADIO!" she shouted over the thundering piano music. "*ISN'T IT? ROGER? WHAT'S HAPPENING* HERE?"

Dad shook his head and pushed the door open. The music stopped just as fast as it had started. The air turned still and quiet. We all looked at each other, not saying a word, as the waves washed up on the rocks, the wind chime rattled and the seagulls screamed.

Mom took a deep breath. "I'm *sure* that there is a perfectly *reasonable*, and *scientific* explanation for what just happened here," she said.

I didn't believe her.

We all stayed close together as we crowded into a dim living room, covered in grungy flowered wallpaper. "Look, *there's* a piano," I finally said, pointing. We gathered around a big old piano pushed against one wall. It was coated with dust and cobwebs.

"Okay, *that* was just creepy," Alondra whimpered. "This thing hasn't been touched in *years*. Can we go home *now?*"

"This old piano has always been here as long as I can remember," Dad said slowly, shaking his head. "Uncle Zack didn't know how to play it, though. He said that it had belonged to one of the lighthouse keepers."

"It looks like a…a beautiful antique," Mom stammered. "And that stone fireplace is stunning. But whatever just happened outside…Roger, we need to think about this." She shuddered and went in the kitchen as the rest of us looked around the messy little living room, trying to calm down.

Alondra turned around and gasped, then wrinkled her nose at a stuffed seagull sitting on a shelf, staring at her with its dusty glass eyes. "Dad? Is *that* thing *real?*"

Dad walked over and smoothed down the seagull's ragged feathers. "It was at one time. This must've been Uncle Zack's seagull."

"His *seagull?*" Alondra said.

"Sure. Everyone in town knew about Uncle Zack's pet seagull. He had found it wounded, with a broken wing, and he nursed it back to health. But it could never fly again, so he kept it as a pet. It followed him around everywhere he went."

"That's *so* cool," I said.

Mom frowned at me. "Don't get any ideas, Dylan."

"That's really disgusting," Alondra said. "I *hate* seagulls. They're filthy and they carry germs."

Dad sighed. "Alondra, is there *anything* in this world that you don't hate?"

Alondra pouted and plopped down on a raggedy old plaid couch by the fireplace. She pointed at an even older-looking TV in a wooden case. "That TV is *ancient*," she grumbled. "I bet that it doesn't even work."

I shrugged and knelt in front of some shelves that sagged with piles of worn-out books. Uncle Zack sure left a lot of them behind. He seemed to like books about bugs, and gardening. And western stories. There were *lots* of those.

"Oh, a wild rose," Mom called from the kitchen. "It looks like it was just picked. Thank you, Roger, that was sweet of you."

"But -"

"Where did you *get* it?" Mom continued, as she walked out of the kitchen holding a big pink flower. "And how did you sneak into the kitchen without us seeing you?"

Dad looked confused. "What do you mean? I've been here in the living room with the kids all this time."

Mom held the flower out to him. "This was on the kitchen table. You didn't leave it there?"

"Noooo," Dad said. He looked as baffled as she did.

Mom stared at the flower for a moment and shook her head. Then she set it down and scurried from window to window, raising the shades and pushing aside the thick curtains.

Since this was a lighthouse keeper's house next to the ocean, I thought that we'd find sailor's charts and pictures of ships on the walls. Instead, we found...*dead butterflies.* Their wings were stretched out and pinned inside some picture frames hanging on the wall. "Luna moth," I read on the label under a huge green one. "Monarch...Tiger Swallowtail..." I read down the rows of butterflies, ignoring the scientific names underneath. Then I found another board that had different kinds of beetles pinned to it. "This house is like a *museum!*"

"No, this house is just *sickening*," Alondra said. "Dad, what are we *doing* here? First we find a...*haunted* piano, a dead bird, and now a...*graveyard* for *insects*..."

She was right. The fireplace mantel...the bookcases... the top of the piano...they were all covered with dusty jars of liquid. I looked closer. The jars were all labeled, and each had some kind of a dead bug inside. "*Gross*," I said. I saw a giant cockroach, and a grub worm as big as Dad's thumb. There were inch-long June bugs, and big black beetles with long antennas that curled over their backs. There were red-eyed cicadas, wasps and ladybugs, a dragonfly, praying mantis, crickets and grasshoppers...there were even some caterpillars and big black ants. "Why are all these *bugs* in here?"

"Uncle Zack was an amateur entomologist – a bug scientist," Dad said. "He was a beekeeper, too – he always had some hives in the backyard, and sold honey at a shop in town. He loved insects."

Mom frowned. "He couldn't have loved them that much, if he drowned them in jars and pinned them to boards." She shivered. "Those poor butterflies."

Mom held up a jar and squinted at the label. A cluster of fat, white maggots and decaying flies floated around in the cloudy liquid. "Roger, this is disgusting! *The Life Cycle of the Blowfly?* Really?" She put the jar down and hid her face in her hands. "This is *not* what I was expecting. When you told me about this place, you made it sound like a nice, quaint beach cottage, straight out of a seascape painting. Instead, you brought us to this...this *nightmare*, this...*house* of *horrors*..."

"Rorianne, you're being unreasonable. I'll donate the insects to the science center first thing in the morning. After they're out of here, you'll see that it's a perfectly normal house underneath."

Mom sighed. "Alondra, I take back what I said in the car. Your uncle *was* weird."

"Now, Rorianne -" Dad said.

"Dylan and Alondra, why don't you get your things and go upstairs to pick out your rooms." Mom sounded very tired. "Your father and I have things to discuss."

"The stairs are this way," Dad said, leading us through the kitchen. It looked as gloomy as the living room, with a dirty table covered with old newspapers and empty cans. The ceiling light hummed and flickered with a weak yellow glow as a fly buzzed around inside, tapping against the glass trying to find a way out. Soon it fell to the bottom of the light, joining the other dead flies that had been trapped inside.

Alondra and I passed a back door at the bottom of the stairs. I stood there and listened as Mom and Dad started talking just around the corner.

"This house doesn't look like it's been redecorated – or *cleaned* – since the 1970's," Mom said. "Zack didn't like to throw anything away, did he?"

"Now Rorianne, it could be worse. At least we have a bathroom upstairs. Those old light keepers had to use a privy out back..."

"Dylan, come on!" Alondra whispered. I hurried to catch up and we carried our suitcases up the stairs to a dark hallway.

Our apartment back home was bright and modern, with white walls and lots of windows. I had never seen anything like *this* place. Drawings of spiders decorated the peeling wallpaper in the hallway. The spiders seemed to crawl up and down the walls and hide under the wood up near the ceiling.

Alondra shivered. "Just looking at that makes me itch," she said. "Who would put *spider* wallpaper in their house?"

I shrugged and peeked into the bathroom at the top of the stairs. I was glad that we didn't have to use an outhouse, like Dad had said.

I opened the door next to the bathroom, and we looked inside...

And we screamed, slammed the door, and dropped our bags on the floor as we ran for the stairs.

"Did you *see* that?" Alondra cried.

I nodded, shaking and looking back at the closed door.

The room was filled with *people!* Dozens of them, staring at us from every direction! "*People,*" I whispered.

"Are you guys alright up there?" Dad called.

"Dad, this room is really weird," Alondra said.

"Oh, you mean the portrait room?" I heard Dad laugh. "Go on in. That's just one of Uncle Zack's collections."

"*Pictures?*" I moaned. I was so embarrassed.

"We are *so* dumb," Alondra said. "We're afraid of a bunch of stupid *paintings!*"

We threw open the door and marched inside, laughing. It was chilly in there, colder than the rest of the house. It felt nice.

Alondra laid her luggage on a big bed that took up half the room. I just looked around.

This bedroom was the *strangest* place I'd ever seen. Every wall was covered with paintings of frowning people in old-time clothes. Their eyes seemed to follow us around the room, watching us wherever we went.

Underneath the creepy paintings was fuzzy red wallpaper with big yellow roses, and naked baby angels with bows and arrows. The wallpaper was all peeling away and hanging from the wall in torn-up strips, falling over some of the picture frames.

"This room is like...like being trapped inside of a Valentine's Day card," I said.

"No, it's more like being trapped inside of a fishbowl, with all these people staring at us."

"But they're, um...just pictures. They can't *see* us."

"In this crazy house, nothing would surprise me."

I stared at her. "And you think *I'm* weird?"

Alondra climbed up on the big bed and unzipped one of her bags. "Dylan, why don't you check out that other room, and see if it's any better than this. I'm going to stay here a minute and cool off. There must be air conditioning in here."

I grabbed my bags and tried the other door down the hall. It was locked, so I went downstairs to find Dad. He and Mom were still talking in low voices, looking annoyed at each other.

"Dad, the other door is locked."

Dad nodded. "That room at the end of the hall was always locked up, even when Uncle Zack lived here. He, um...never told us why." Dad dug around in his pocket. "Here's a skeleton key," he said, as he handed it to me. "It'll unlock every door in the house."

Back upstairs, I saw Alondra still lying down beside her bags, so I ignored her and tried the strange old key in the door down the hall. It swung open with a loud squeak.

As I stepped inside, strings of dusty cobwebs swayed in the air as they dangled from the ceiling and brushed against my face. A fat spider dropped onto my head. I shrieked and swatted it away, its body landing on the floor with a tiny click. The spider scurried off as I shuddered and looked around the room.

Cobwebs covered the walls and furniture like thick gray fishing nets. Shadows loomed in the corners, the sunlight blocked by black-speckled curtains that had been drawn tight over the window.

The cobwebs were creepy, but I didn't see any reason for the room to be locked up. It looked ordinary, nothing like the portrait room. The high ceiling slanted down to low walls at each end of the room. Shiny brown wooden planks covered the walls and ceiling, making the room look like a cabin on an old ship. A high, narrow bed was pushed against one of the low walls, near the window. On one side of the door was a long dresser with a mirror over it, and on the other side was a big old-fashioned desk. A huge, brown leather chair sat in the corner near the bed.

I liked it.

I went over and sat on the bed, bouncing on it to see how soft it was. The springs squeaked and a big cloud of dust floated up from the ratty old blue-and-white bedspread. I sneezed. *Everything* in here was covered with dust, even the pictures on the walls. They weren't like the colorful pictures of flowers and stuff that Mom painted. These were darker, brown and gray pictures of ships in stormy seas, or of old-time fishermen pulling in nets.

I got up and wandered over to the dresser, looking at a model clipper ship that sat below the mirror. On one side of the ship were a big white bowl and a pitcher that held nothing but some dead flies. Near that I found an old coffee mug with a chipped handle and a stubby little brush inside, like one that Mom would use to power her face.

I knelt down and pulled open the dresser drawers, but was disappointed when I found them all empty. I was about to snoop around in the desk when Alondra and Dad came in.

"Ugh! Those cobwebs are *so* gross. And what *is* that on those curtains – *mildew?*" Alondra turned and poked at a kerosene lamp that was sitting on the desk. "I hope there's electricity in here."

"*Yes*, there's electricity, Alondra," Dad said. He looked at the bare light bulb hanging down from a wire in the ceiling. "That will need to be fixed, though. It's a fire hazard. In the meantime, try not to use it, okay, Dylan? Just use that lamp beside your bed."

"Sure, Dad," I said, as I listened to Mom heading up the creaky wooden stairs.

"Oh, *my!* This is just *dreadful!*"

"Your mother must've discovered the portrait room," Dad said.

"And the spiders," Alondra mumbled. "You know how Mom hates spiders."

"I'm sure that wallpaper will be the first thing to go," Dad said. "Along with those paintings in your room."

But when Mom saw *my* room, she smiled and clasped her hands in front of her. "Now, *this* is the way I pictured the house! It's like it was frozen in time. And this *furniture!* These look like *real* antiques!"

"They look like real *junk*, if you ask me," Alondra muttered.

"No, these are lovely. Look at this old iron bed and this quilt, the roll-top desk, this big leather chair…this room looks like it hasn't been touched in years." Mom ran her finger through the dust on top of the dresser. "This all needs dusting and vacuuming, though. And furniture polish. And you'll need some fresh sheets and blankets for that bed. Oh, and Roger, you'll need to open that window; it's so musty in here."

Dad went to the window and parted the torn curtains. They fell apart as soon as he touched them, drifting to the floor like tissue.

"And you'll need new curtains," Alondra said, wrinkling up her nose.

"I don't need *curtains*. Who's going to look in?"

"You're getting new curtains, Dylan," Mom said in her no-nonsense voice. "Now, did you find anything interesting in here?"

"Not really, except that ship on the dresser, and that big pitcher and coffee mug. Some lady left her makeup brush in it."

"That bowl and pitcher is what people used for a sink before there was running water. And that's not a coffee mug; it's an old shaving mug and brush. This was obviously a man's room."

"*Obviously*, Mom," Alondra said. "No *woman* would want to sleep in this rat hole. It looks like a cave in here."

"No it doesn't. *I* want to sleep here."

"Dylan, are you sure?" Mom asked. "Your sister is right; this room is so gloomy."

I shrugged. "I'm sure. It beats that girly wallpaper with the naked babies."

Alondra rolled her eyes. "Those are *cupids*, Dylan. They are not *naked babies*."

"Whatever. Either way, you can have 'em."

She frowned. "So, I guess I'm taking the portrait room. But at least there's air conditioning in there."

"But Alondra, there's no air conditioning in the house," Mom said.

"But it's *freezing* in there. It feels good. Go in there and see."

She and Mom headed for the other room. I was just showing Dad the ship on the dresser when we heard Alondra shriek down the hall.

"I'm telling you, it was *cold* in here just a minute ago!"

"I better see what's going on," Dad said. I followed him down the hall and looked in Alondra's room. Nothing had changed, except now it was just as hot as the rest of the house. Mom and Dad just stared at her as she wailed about how hot it was, and how much she hated it here and wanted to go home.

So, Alondra got stuck with the room with the scary portraits and weird wallpaper. It wasn't air conditioned, either. She was having a fit! I was glad. I went down the hall to my room and started unpacking my things with a big smile.

I dumped my clothes into the dresser drawers and put my toothbrush in the bathroom. All that was left was just my radio, some computer games, and books. I looked at the book covers as I pulled them out of my backpack: *Illustrated Guide to Dogs, Sailing Ships of the World*, the Maine book that Dad gave me, and my favorite adventure novels and superhero comics. Dad had told me that I didn't need to bring them since there was a library in town, but those were my favorites and I read them all the time.

I sighed. I knew that Mom worried about me because I liked to stay in my room by myself and read books, instead of going outside to play with friends. I always tried to tell her that I *liked* reading books.

But I never told her that I had no friends.

I was the smallest kid in my class. I *hated* it. Everyone thought that I was seven or eight, instead of ten. The other boys in my class laughed at me because I couldn't shoot a basketball or throw a football as well as they could, just because they were bigger. They thought that I couldn't do *anything* right.

Once, I asked if I could join them when they were playing basketball. They just told me that I throw like a *girl*, and to go home and play with my *dolls*. When I told them that I didn't play with dolls, they tried to beat me up. Why would Mom think that I'd want to play with *them?* It was easier to just stay home by myself, unless I went out with Dad on his sailboat.

Every weekend, Dad took me to the marina where he kept his sailboat, the *Rorianne Rose*. I always felt better when I went out sailing with him. Out on his boat, I felt...free. Like nobody could ever make fun of me out there. Like I could do *anything*, and it didn't matter how small I was. Dad wasn't very big, either, but he had strong hands and arm muscles from his years of working at the boat shop. I hoped that I would be like him when I grew up.

One day when we were sailing on the Hudson River, I told Dad about the boys on the basketball court. "Well, just because you might not be good at those things *now*, doesn't mean you'll never be," Dad had said, in his quiet voice. "But so what? I bet that those boys can't sail a *boat* without tipping it over."

That was the way Dad was. He always knew how to make me feel better. In fact, he was my best friend. But that didn't count, since he was my dad.

I tried to forget about the bullies as I stacked the books on the desk and started snooping around in the cubbyholes inside. My fingers brushed against a piece of thick paper that was stuck in the back. I pulled it out, trying not to rip it.

It was an old, faded, black-and-white picture of a skinny guy standing on the deck of a boat and grinning at the camera. He wore big boots and held some heavy-looking fishing nets, even though he didn't look much older than Alondra. There was another man sitting behind him, with a thick mustache and a hat pulled low over his forehead.

It was an interesting picture. I turned it over and squinted at the faded handwriting on the back. "M.M. 1888," I read out loud. *Who was M.M.?* I wondered. I took the picture over to the dresser so I could stick it on the mirror.

CLUMP...CLUMP...CREEEEAK...

I gasped and looked up as footsteps crossed my room, stepping on the squeaky floorboard near the bed. Something blocked the sunlight coming in the window. I dropped the picture on the dresser and stared into the mirror at a long-legged figure standing behind me. I couldn't see its face...but it seemed to be watching me.

"Dad?" I said, spinning around in my chair. But Dad wasn't there, and the person was gone.

"Dylan, do you want to come down here?" Dad called. "We're heading out to see the lighthouse. We need to hurry; it'll be getting dark soon."

The *lighthouse?* I'd been waiting all *day* to see the lighthouse! I grinned and forgot about the person in the mirror as I ran downstairs to join Dad, Mom, and Alondra.

It was a long walk up the winding lighthouse stairs, but we had plenty of times to catch our breath. That was because Mom and Dad had to stop at every landing to baby Alondra along, who refused to look out the windows, or even down at her feet.

"I can't believe that I'm letting you drag me up here," she whined. "You know that I can't stand heights."

"Well, don't stop now, because we're almost at the top. And your father said that the view is unbelievable."

"But we can only go up as far as this railing here, just below the lantern room," Dad said. He opened a door onto the balcony at the lighthouse top. "We're not allowed to go in there or touch any of the equipment, because this is still a working lighthouse. Those are off-limits to all of us."

As we stepped outside, the lighthouse's bright spotlight circled around just above our heads. Its beam shown far out into the bay, where a sailboat headed for the harbor under the pink and purple sky.

Mom gasped. "Oh, *Roger.* You were right; this is *gorgeous!* Alondra, honey, you *really* should open your eyes and see this sunset."

"Yeah, isn't this great? I remember that Uncle Zack let my friends and me come up here sometimes. On a clear day, you can see all the way to Canada."

Alondra looked like she didn't care. She just stood frozen with her back against the wall, her eyes closed and hair blowing across her face.

I left Mom and Dad and wandered over to the other side of the tower. It was *cold* up here. It wasn't just the wind, either. The air all around me felt like a winter day, even though it was the end of June.

I looked down at the rocks below the lighthouse, and out at the town across the bay. I wondered how high up we were. Dad said that the lighthouse was fifty feet tall, though *we* weren't at the very top. I leaned against the railing and kicked my feet up behind me, balancing on my stomach…

Two hands grabbed my waist and pulled me off the railing, setting me on my feet beside the wall. I looked around for Dad or Mom, but I was alone.

"No playing on the lighthouse!" a man growled.

"OK, Dad," I shouted.

"Did you say something, Dylan?" Dad called.

"Uh…nothing…"

I looked around again, puzzled. I was still alone. Dad, Mom, and Alondra were on the other side of the tower.

If *Dad* wasn't the one who pulled me off the railing and yelled at me, then who was?

CHAPTER 3

Mysteries

I didn't tell anyone about the voice I'd heard at the lighthouse top, or the hands that pulled me away from the railing. And I didn't tell anyone about that old picture I had found in the desk. I had left it on the dresser, but when we got back from the lighthouse, it was back in its cubbyhole where I had found it.

I thought about those things as Mom changed the sheets and blankets on my bed, and made me vacuum all the dust and cobwebs out of my room. I waited until Alondra went to bed and Mom was in the shower, and then I crept downstairs. I was glad that I had a chance to talk to Dad alone.

"Dad?" I whispered. "I think there was someone in my room."

Dad didn't even seem surprised. "What makes you say that?" he said.

"Well, um…when we came back in from looking at the lighthouse, all the books on my desk were knocked over. One was open, like somebody had been reading it."

I looked at him. He just looked down at his hands, like he was thinking hard about something. "Go on," he said.

"Um…my radio was on, too, and it was playing…*classical* music. I don't listen to classical music."

"Well, there are different radio stations here. It could have been just picking up a different signal."

I shrugged. "But Dad, the weirdest thing was that I saw someone in the mirror. He was standing behind me, but when I turned around, he wasn't there."

"I see." Dad nodded. "Do you feel comfortable about staying in that room?"

"I guess. Why wouldn't I be?"

"That's my boy!" Dad said with a smile as he sent me back toward the stairs. "Dylan, I don't think you have anything to worry about. Maybe you just didn't remember looking at your book, and leaving the radio on. And you're in an unfamiliar place; some of those shadows could've looked like a person standing there. I'm sure that it's all a coincidence, and things will look different in the morning. Have a good night's rest, son."

It wasn't a shadow, I thought. I should've known that he wouldn't believe me. "Thanks, Dad…I think," I mumbled as I plodded back up the stairs.

As I laid in bed that night, I tried not to think about my conversation with Dad. I was sure that he knew something he wasn't telling me.

I watched as the rotten curtains blew in the warm breeze that came into my room. I had never been able to sleep with my window open before. My bedroom window back home faced a brick wall, but the window in *this* room faced the ocean and lighthouse. Across the bay, I could see some lights from town. Every few seconds, the lighthouse beam would flash into my window and sweep across the bedroom walls, like a ghost. I rolled over and faced the wall so the light wouldn't keep shining in my eyes.

It was so *quiet* here. I finally fell asleep to the sound of crickets chirping in the lawn, and the *shhhhhhhh* sound of the ocean washing up on the rocks.

***

"THERE'S A *MAN* IN MY ROOM!"

I sat up in bed as Alondra's scream echoed down the hall. She wouldn't stop screeching even as Mom and Dad rushed upstairs and tried to calm her down.

"...HE WAS HERE! HE WAS *WATCHING* MEEEE!"

I could hear Alondra sobbing as a gust of cold air blew through my room and footsteps clattered across the wooden floor. When the lighthouse beam flashed into my window, I saw my ceiling light swinging back and forth on its cord as the closet door rattled and swung shut. I pulled my blanket up to my chin and stared at the swaying lightbulb.

"Mom, Dad, what's *happening* here?" I shouted.

Dad didn't answer as he threw my door open, grabbed me up out of bed, tossed me over his shoulder and took off back down the stairs. "Dad, put me *down!* What are you *doing?*"

He set me on my feet and pointed at the porch. "Dylan, you go with your mother and sister! You all need to get out of the house, *now!* Get in the car and lock the doors! I'll be right behind you."

I looked back at Dad as he grabbed the phone and punched in 911. "Yes, we need the police right away! My daughter just saw a stranger in her bedroom..."

Soon Dad joined us in the car as we waited for the cops to show up. Alondra just kept on blubbering and begging Dad to take us to a hotel. I think Mom agreed with her, but didn't say so.

"Thank goodness," Mom said, as a police car pulled into the driveway a few minutes later. Two tired-looking cops got out and started asking questions.

"Can you tell us what he looked like?" they asked Alondra.

"I don't *know!* He left so *fast!*" she whimpered, wiping a tear from her eye. "But he was wearing some kind of a blue uniform."

"Like a cop?" I asked.

"No, like a...I don't *know* what. But he was looking at the stuff on my dresser. Then he looked at *me!*" Alondra shivered. "I screamed, and he disappeared. Then I don't know *where* he went. He could be *anywhere.*"

"Did you notice anything missing?"

"As a matter of fact...my cosmetics! I had some on the dresser, and now they're *gone!*"

The policemen glanced at each other, and stared at the house. They seemed a little nervous as they crept up to the front door with their guns drawn. I wondered why they were nervous. They had guns, didn't they?

We all sat in the locked car and I kept watching the house, but never spotted anyone trying to sneak away.

"Well, we found no signs of an intruder," one cop told us when they finally came back. "We searched every room and closet, the basement...even under the beds. It's safe to return."

"Thank you, Officers," Mom said. "We were so sorry to call you out here in the middle of the night."

"This isn't the first time that this has happened here, ma'am. You must be the newcomers. Everyone in town knows about *this* place."

"But my *dad's* not a new -"

"Dylan, shush." Mom frowned at me.

I knew that the cops were watching us as we headed back inside. "*That* is one *freaky* house," I heard one tell the other, before they drove away.

***

"That's the last one," Dad was telling Mom as I went downstairs the next morning. I guessed that he had gotten up early and packed up Uncle Zack's jars of insects. Five big boxes stood by the front door, but the living room shelves were bare. "This is a remarkably good collection of specimens. The Science Center will be glad to get them."

"I don't care what you do with them, Roger. Just get rid of them, and don't bring them back!"

I fixed myself a bowl of cereal as Dad started carrying the boxes out to the car. "How do you feel, Dylan?" Mom asked. "Did you sleep okay after what happened last night?"

"I'm okay." I shrugged and dragged my spoon through my cereal. It was gross. It was some kind of health cereal that Mom bought, and it always got soggy and soft.

"What about *me*?" Alondra snapped. "*I* was the one who had some creepy guy in my room, watching me! I can't believe that you're all so calm when there was a *burglar* in here last night!"

"Alondra, you heard the officers. It was an unexplained incident. There was nobody there."

"Mom, you don't *understand!*" Alondra pouted down into her breakfast bowl. "I *hate* this place. I want to go home. It's so *boring* here."

Mom raised her eyebrows. "*Boring?* You just said that there was a strange man in your room, and we had to call the police out here in the middle of the night. Do you think that's *boring?* How much more excitement do you want?"

"You *know* what I mean!" Alondra cried. "Dad and Dylan have their sailboats, and you have your painting. But there's nothing for *me* to do here!"

"Don't let your father hear you say that, or he'll put you to work," Mom said. "There's plenty of yard work and cleaning up to do around here. And remember, I've already offered to teach you to paint, and I'm sure that your father would take you out on the boat if you ask him. There's no excuse for you to be bored."

Alondra rolled her eyes. "*Fine*, Mother. Get me a box. I suppose I'll pack up all these tacky knick-knacks. But that stuffed seagull over there is going *straight* to the dump."

"No, *no!*" I cried. "I like that seagull. I'll bring it up to my room."

"*See*, Mom? Now he's putting dead animals in his room. I *told* you he was weird."

"Who's weird?" Dad asked as he came back inside.

"It's okay, Roger. We were just having a discussion."

"I *know*," Dad muttered, frowning at Alondra. "Dylan, why don't you help me bring these boxes out to the car, and we'll take a ride into town. I think your mother and sister need to have a *good, long talk.*"

As Dad and I drove through town, I ate a frosted doughnut that Dad bought me at the gas station, while he pointed out all the places he remembered. There wasn't much to see. We passed a diner, a little supermarket that Dad called a "general store," a laundromat, post office, antique shop, a boarded-up movie theater and a library, a big old hotel that Dad called a "bed-and-breakfast," and the smallest school that I had ever seen. There was an ice cream shop where Dad said he used to go when he was my age, but it was empty and had a "for sale" sign out front.

Dad even showed me the house where he grew up. Grandma and Grandpa Flint had lived there until they moved to a condo down south, back before I was born. I didn't like their house as much as our cottage, but I didn't tell Dad that.

There were a lot of abandoned houses in town, with over-grown grass and broken windows, and falling-down porches and roofs. I told Dad that it would be fun to explore them, but he just looked sad.

"The town wasn't always like this," he mumbled. "But you'll like the Science Center, where we're bringing Uncle Zack's collection. They have a whale skeleton, an aquarium with a live octopus, and tanks with other sea creatures that you can touch. The place has been there since I was a kid."

But Dad was wrong. We parked in front of a building with boarded-up windows. It looked like it had been empty for years. "This...*was* the Science Center," Dad said, staring at the dingy brick wall. He sighed and started the car.

"So, what do you think they did with the whale and the octopus?"

Dad just shrugged. He looked as disappointed as I felt. "Your mother won't be happy about this," he said as we headed home with the boxes of bugs.

***

Dad was right: Mom was annoyed when she saw us carrying the boxes down to the basement, but I guess she knew that there was nothing we could do about it. She sighed and slammed her way back into the living room with her cleaning stuff. She said that she couldn't even *think* of working on her paintings when the house was such a mess.

I wasn't going to stay inside, though. I wanted to explore the rocky beach that Dad told me was at the bottom of the cliff. The beach was only there at low tide. It was under water at high tide, and I wasn't allowed to go down there then.

I looked down over the cliff, past the path that led to the water. The foamy waves lapped against the rocks, looking safe enough, but the beach was nowhere in sight. It was high tide. I sighed and headed back to the house.

I found Dad on the front porch, scraping the peeling paint off the wood around the windows. A new paintbrush and can of white paint sat by the door. "Can I help?" I asked.

"Sure," Dad said, handing me the paint scraper. "I'll go and get the other scraper out of my toolbox, if you want to finish up this window."

I finished chipping off the old paint, and thought I did a good job, too, but Dad sounded puzzled when he came back out on the porch. "Dylan, what did you do with the paint?"

"The paint? What do you mean?"

"The paint and brush that I had right here by the door. It's *gone!* You know that I want to try and get this painted before it rains."

"But I didn't *do* anything with the paint, Dad! I was over here the whole time you were gone. See, I'm done with my window. I didn't even go *near* the paint!"

"Then you need to help me find it, and stop playing games. You must know where it is, Dylan. It didn't walk off by itself."

I was mad that Dad blamed me for hiding his paint, like a stupid little kid. What would I hide his paint for? If I wanted to play a trick on him, I could think of better things than that.

Dad searched under the front porch and in the shed as I looked around the yard. I finally spotted the missing paint can near the driveway. "Dad! It's over here!"

Dad gasped. "What in the world -"

We both stared down at a line of white spots and splatters that speckled the grass, all the way from the driveway to the lighthouse. Paint dripped over the sides of the can and gummed up the bristles of the new paintbrush that lay across the open top.

"Look at this mess, Dylan!" Dad barked. "A brand-new gallon of paint, wasted! Is this your idea of a joke? Huh?"

"But I didn't *take* it, Dad! I didn't *put* it there!"

Dad took a deep breath. "Dylan, my car keys are on the table. Why don't you go get the metal detector out of the trunk, and try it out?"

"But Dad, don't you *believe* me?"

"I don't know what to believe right now," he grumbled. "This has me baffled, and I need time to think. Now, go look for the treasure. I'll do the work myself."

I got the car keys and headed out to get the metal detector. I'd rather look for the treasure than paint the house, anyway.

Dad had always told me the legend of Captain Cutlass the Pirate. His buried treasure has never been found. Mom said that that was all it was - a legend - and there was no such thing as a buried pirate treasure nowadays. But Dad believed the old stories that said it was buried here. He and his friends had searched for it when they were kids, but never found any sign of it. Dad wasn't going to give up, though. He had bought the metal detector and showed me how to use it, and promised that he'd help me search for the treasure this summer.

As I started wandering back and forth across the yard, I thought about the story I had read in Dad's Maine book. I knew it by heart:

'Captain Cutlass was one of the most terrifying and infamous pirates in history. He and his crew of bloodthirsty scoundrels prowled the seas for over ten years, robbing ships and showing no mercy toward their victims. Armed ships were finally sent to capture him. After a fierce battle with many casualties on both sides, Cutlass and his remaining men were taken prisoner and hanged for their misdeeds. His buried treasure, which has never been found, is believed to be hidden somewhere along the coast of Maine...'

I forgot all about the mystery of the paint as I daydreamed about finding Captain Cutlass's treasure. It was going to make me *so* rich!

***

Is it always so foggy and rainy here? I wondered. I had hardly even had time to start looking for the treasure, when the rain started and Mom called me back in the house. Soon the fog was so thick that I couldn't see the town across the bay.

I flopped down on my bed, listening to the rain pounding on the roof. I had already read through my stack of books from home. And I knew that if I went downstairs to watch TV, Mom would tell me to help her clean the house.

I looked over at the clipper ship on the dresser, and thought about that old picture of the guy on the boat. It might be fun to check out the attic storeroom to see what else I could find. I snuck downstairs and grabbed a flashlight out of the pantry.

Dad had told us that the attic door was in the back of the hall closet. Some of Uncle Zack's clothes still hung there on their rusty hangers: patched old pants, checkered shirts, and even his white beekeeper's suit. I parted the clothes and pushed open the attic door. It smelled funny in there, like mice and mushrooms and moldy old papers.

The attic roof slanted all the way down to the floor. Even I had to bend over to fit through the little door, as I shined my flashlight into the dark room. Dust and cobwebs covered piles of catalogues that were stacked everywhere on the floor, the pages chewed by mice and stuck together from the damp air. I sat down and looked at a catalog from 1978. It was filled with pictures of fruit trees and flowers and all kinds of vegetables. I tossed it back on its pile and then flipped through some old magazines about "homesteading" and "organic" gardening, whatever they were.

I was disappointed that I didn't find any more old pictures, or antique junk like the stuff in my room. I was about to leave when I noticed a big trunk sitting off by itself in the darkest corner.

I crawled over and blew the dust off the trunk. When I opened it, thick cobwebs tore away from the lid and dangled from the rafters above my head. Spiders crept back up their broken webs and disappeared under the ceiling boards.

I tried not to think about the spiders as I shined my light in the trunk. It was almost empty, except for a little wooden box and a scuffed leather case lying in one corner, and an ordinary notebook in the other.

The Journal of Zachary Flint, it read, written in faded black marker on the worn-out green cover. That might be interesting. I flipped through it and found that it was filled with Uncle Zack's messy handwriting, and little doodles and diagrams. I set it on the floor to read later, and lifted out the leather case. There was an old pair of binoculars inside. They weren't like Dad's modern ones; these were bigger, and heavier than they looked. I put their soft leather strap around my neck and hung them over my back as I pulled out the little box. It held a brass compass that was still shiny, even after being stored for so long. It looked even older than the binoculars, but still worked, pointing the way north with a carved silver arrow. My flashlight glinted on two letters engraved at the top: *M.M.* They were the same letters that were on the back of that old picture!

SQUEEEAK...

The attic door swung shut.

"Mom? Dad? I'm in here!" I called.

There was no answer. The rain beat on the roof, drowning out any voices or footsteps from the rest of the house.

"Alondra?" I shined my flashlight at the door. There was nothing there except the dust floating through the air and cobwebs swaying from the rafters.

The door rattled and the whole room went cold.

Someone started breathing beside me – loud.

A pile of catalogues slid to the floor, followed by a second one and a third...

...and my flashlight dimmed and went out, leaving me alone in the dark.

I grabbed the binocular case, compass, and notebook, scrambled to the attic door, and burst into the warm hallway. I slammed the door without looking back and fled to my room, where I tossed the things on my bed and tried to figure out what just happened.

I didn't tell Mom or Dad about it. Mom wouldn't believe me anyway, so I just picked up Uncle Zack's journal and started to read.

It was boring. I had hoped to read about his pet seagull. Instead, it was just a lot of dull records about his garden and bees. He wrote about what he planted each year, how long it took for the plants to grow, and the dates when he started picking his crops. But between all the garden stories were notes that kept me reading until I finished the end of the book.

The Journal of Zachary Flint, 1982 – 1984:

...Full moon last night. As usual, I got no sleep. I really need to get rid of that old piano one of these days...
...Footsteps upstairs again...
...Cannot heat the living room, no matter how high I stoke the fire...
...Sometimes I think that I share the house with an unseen companion. I try not to think about the ghost stories...

***

It stopped raining after dinner that night. As the sun set behind the woods, the clouds blew away and left a clear pink sky. I was glad that the rain stopped. Dad had promised that he'd take me sailing the next day, and I didn't want anything to ruin it. We sat on the porch and watched as the stars came out, while a warm breeze rustled the grass that still needed mowing.

I had brought the binoculars, compass, and Uncle Zack's journal downstairs to show Dad. He told me that the binoculars and compass were antiques, so I had to be careful with them. Then I watched as he flipped through the old notebook.

"I remember these journals," Dad said. "Uncle Zack was always writing about his garden and bees; they were his pride and joy. There were other journals where he wrote about his seagull, and his insect studies, too."

"You mean, there's more than one book?"

"There *was*. But they could've gotten ruined, or thrown out by now. You're lucky that you found this one."

I didn't tell Dad, but I decided to search the house for the rest of Uncle Zack's journals. I had the whole summer to find them, but there was *no* way that I was ever going into that attic storeroom again!

After everyone went to bed, I stood at my window and looked out at the ocean, while the circling lighthouse beam lit up the sky for miles around. I wanted to try out those old binoculars. I hung the strap around my neck and looked over at the boats in the harbor, bobbing under the moonlight. I could see the craters on the moon, the lights of a ship far out in the open sea...and two men standing by the lighthouse!

I put the binoculars down and watched as the glowing tips of their cigarettes moved through the darkness. One guy nudged the other and they both looked up through their own binoculars, straight at my window...

I gasped and ducked out of sight. Could they really *see* me up here? I had to go tell Dad –

"GET OUT!"

I jumped as a man's voice boomed across the yard. It didn't sound like Dad. It was louder and deeper, echoing from every direction. Then I remembered: it was the same voice that I had heard at the top of the lighthouse!

My heart thudded as I peeked up over the windowsill and put the binoculars to my eyes. The men were sprinting away, shouting to each other, as a glowing ball of light zoomed across the field and chased them toward the cliff. The light circled around them and faded as they disappeared down the path.

The binoculars bounced against my back as I bolted down the stairs to the kitchen door. I yanked it open and jumped down on the deck, looking all around at the empty, moonlit yard.

"Dad?" I called. I expected to see him heading back to the house with a flashlight, but I was alone. The two men were gone, and so was the ball of light. The waves washed up on the rocks and crickets chirped in the grass. It was just like it had never happened.

"Dylan, what are you doing out here?"

"*Dad!*" I spun around, surprised, as Dad shuffled out of the kitchen and switched on the back light, yawning and scratching his beard, like he had just woken up. "Dad, there was somebody outside, *spying* on us! I thought you were out here chasing them with a flashlight, but -"

"Young man, you need to get back inside. You can't be wandering around out here at this time of night."

"But there was *someone out here*, Dad! A man yelled at them, but it didn't sound like you. And then -"

"It must've been a dream. You can tell me all about it in the morning."

"It *wasn't* a *dream!*"

Dad sighed. "Okay, then. If it wasn't a dream, I'll call the sheriff first thing tomorrow, and tell him what you saw." He took my shoulder and steered me back into the house. "Now, you need to go back to bed before you wake up everyone else. It's late, and we all need to get some sleep."

I turned and headed back upstairs, leaving Dad standing in the doorway and staring out into the night.

***

"Those portraits have *got* to go," Alondra said the next morning, as she and Mom looked in at them from her bedroom door. "I can't handle having them looking at me any longer."

"You're right," Mom said. "They're poorly done, and their facial expressions are very disturbing. I'll help you take them down, and bring them to the basement."

I ate a bowl of soggy cereal, watching Mom and Alondra carry the portraits down the basement stairs. It was spooky down there, with dark stone walls, and a big old-fashioned furnace that Dad said was noisy in the winter.

THUMP...THUMP...

I looked over my shoulder as the sound of footsteps and voices drifted from the front porch. It was only Dad, and the same two policemen who were here the other night. The cops asked me what I saw last night, then went back outside to investigate the yard. Meanwhile, I grabbed the old binoculars I'd found, and helped Dad hitch the boat trailer back on the car. We were going to haul my sailboat, *Thunder*, to the harbor for the summer.

When the cops came back, they said they found some fresh cigarette butts beside the lighthouse, but unless I could describe the men, there was nothing they could do.

Before Dad and I left, Mom turned to Alondra and me. "I have a surprise for you two," she said. "There's a pool over at the summer camp where your father used to work. It's open to the public this summer, so we can take you there to go swimming any time you want."

"*Really*, Mom?" Alondra squealed. "Can we go *today*? Like, *now*?"

That was the first time that I had seen Alondra get excited since we moved here! I didn't know why she cared about going to a pool, though. I watched her when we would go to the pool back home in the city. She hardly ever went swimming. She just laid around on her towel and looked at *boys*. How boring!

I shrugged. "Why do we need to go to a *pool* when the *ocean* is right here?"

Mom frowned. "You know that your sister will not swim in a lake or ocean, and neither will I. They're both so dirty and polluted."

"Well, *I* don't want to go to any pool," I said. "Me and Dad are going sailing today, remember?"

"That's *Dad and I*, young man," Mom said. "And you should appreciate that your father and I have found some fun places to take you this summer. However, I know that you and your father have your own plans. Have fun, and be careful. Do *exactly* what your father tells you, and wear your life jacket!"

As Dad and I pulled into the harbor, a pickup truck idled beside the dock, chugging out smelly exhaust fumes. Its bed was loaded with big wire cages that Dad told me were lobster traps, but he didn't let me go look at them. Instead, he introduced me to the harbormaster, and we unloaded *Thunder* into the dock space that Dad had rented. Then we climbed aboard Dad's big boat, *Rorianne Rose*, and headed into the bay.

Dad had built *Rorianne Rose* by himself, and named it after Mom. It was a twenty-four foot sloop that looked like an old-time boat, with little round portholes like an ocean liner. Back home, we would take it out on the Hudson River and stay there the entire day, just looking at the other boats, and the seagulls and birds. Sometimes we would even anchor somewhere overnight, and sleep in the cabin below the deck.

I was the only one who ever went sailing with Dad. Mom was afraid of the ocean, and Alondra hated boats. But then, *Alondra* hated *everything*.

All my life, Dad had taught me about boats and how to sail them. I liked them as much as he did. One time when I was eight years old, Dad dropped his glasses overboard and couldn't see. I had to sail us home. Mom had gotten really mad when she heard that. I didn't know why, since Dad had been right there with me the whole time. But Dad told her that proved I was turning into a real sailor, so that's when he built me *Thunder*.

He gave me *Thunder* for my tenth birthday. It was my most favorite thing that I owned. *Thunder* was shaped just like R*orianne Rose*, except there was no cabin on top.

Back home in the city, I could only take *Thunder* out if Dad was nearby in his boat. But here in Maine, I can go sailing on the bay whenever I want! My only rules were that I had to stay between the lighthouse and town, and to never, *never* go near the cliffs by the lighthouse. And I always had to wear a life jacket, even though I had learned to swim before I could even walk.

Dad wanted to show me the harbor and bay before I took *Thunder* out by myself. He sat in the stern - the back of the boat - with his hand on the tiller. That's the steering bar that's attached to the rudder. Dad usually steered the boat, while I handled the mainsheet - the rope that controls the sail. Dad told me that sailors don't call it a rope, though. It's a *line*. Dad gets annoyed with me if I don't use the right words for the parts of the boat.

We didn't say much as we tacked across the bay, the wind in our hair and sun on our faces. Dad kept us far from shore as we passed by the cliffs. Our lighthouse looked so tiny from the water! I saw someone at the lighthouse top again, but when I looked through the old binoculars, the person was gone. I didn't tell Dad.

Back home in New York, we passed skyscrapers, and big tugboats pulling rusty barges, but it was so *different* here. We saw some funny-looking birds that Dad called *puffins,* and all kinds of other birds that I had never seen before. We even saw a bald eagle! With the binoculars, I spotted whales jumping out of the water, and seals lying on the rocks. We passed rocky islands covered with trees, and lobster fishermen pulling traps out of the water.

"Can we get closer and watch them?" I asked.

Dad shook his head. "They're not out here for fun; they're trying to make a living. We need to stay out of their way."

A few minutes later, Dad pointed at a green mound further out to sea. "See that island over there?" he asked. "That's Rat Island. I'm going to take you out there sometime; it's owned by the state and free for everyone to use."

The wind was to our backs all the way home, making *Rorianne Rose* slice through the waves like a dolphin. Dad and I sang old sea chanties as the spray splashed over the bow and glistened in the air. It made me forget about all the weird stuff happening back at the cottage.

***

Dad and I hadn't been home for long, when Alondra screamed and ran out of her room. "Mom! They're *back!* The *paintings* are *back on the wall!* Where's Dylan? I'm going to *kill* him!"

"But I didn't *do* anything!"

"Look! Just *look* at this!" she cried. "Mom! Dad!"

Dad ran upstairs to see what was going on, and I followed him to Alondra's room. We stood in the doorway and stared at the portraits that all stared right back.

"Your brother is right, Alondra. He couldn't have moved those heavy paintings by himself. It took both you and your mother to lift some of them off the wall."

"Then *who did?*" Alondra yelled.

"I don't know," I said in a small voice. "I saw someone at the top of the lighthouse again today. Maybe it's -"

"Dylan, please!" Mom snapped. "This is very bizarre…"

I watched as the three of them argued about the paintings. *I* didn't know what to think. I had seen Mom and Alondra take them down that morning. They had piled them on a stack of broken old window shutters in the cellar. Then they had gone to the pool while Dad and I were sailing. So what *happened* when we were gone?

This house was getting creepier every day. I was ready to sleep in *Rorianne Rose's* cabin for the rest of the summer!

That night, I stared up at the shiny dark wood on the slanted ceiling and listened to the rain pattering on the roof again. I was glad that we had gone sailing, since the rain was supposed to continue for a while.

I rolled over and faced the wall, tired out from our day on the boat. Mom said it was the sunshine and fresh air that did it. I was almost asleep when…

KNOCK. KNOCK-KNOCK. KNOCK…

"Dylan, stop that!" Alondra yelled.

"I'm not *doing* anything!"

I sat up and looked at the wall that separated our rooms. There it was again – KNOCK-KNOCK-KNOCK – like someone was rapping on the wall with their knuckles.

"Well, *somebody* is doing it. And you better *stop!*"

"*What* is going *on* up here?" Mom and Dad asked as they stormed up the stairs. I crawled out of bed and wandered down the hall to Alondra's room.

The knocking started again, faster and faster, as we all huddled in the doorway and stared at the wall. "Someone...is trying to tell us something," Dad whispered.

"Oh, Roger!" Mom sighed.

"No, Rorianne, listen! That's...Morse Code."

Mom folded her arms. "Roger, who would know *Morse Code* in this day and age?"

"*Me*," Dad said. "Or maybe a pilot, or a seaman...you know, this could even be coming from someone of a different era -"

"Roger, stop being ridiculous!"

"Shhh."

The knocking continued.

"I...am here," Dad translated. "I...am...still...here. I see you. I...am watching you..."

"Stop that, Dad!" Alondra whimpered. "That isn't funny! Now you're just trying to scare us!"

I crept closer to Dad and stared at the spot where the knocking was coming from. "Who's here?" I whispered. "Who's... watching us?"

The knocking began. "M-A-T-T-H..." Dad said.

Mom made a face. "*Math*? That makes no sense. What is that supposed to *mean*?"

Dad shrugged. "I don't know. It just stopped there."

Alondra stomped over to her bed and grabbed her pillow and blankets. "*That's* it! I'm not going to sleep up here with some...*poltergeist*," she muttered. "Who knows? There could even be a whole *family* of them in here..."

"Young lady, there are no *poltergeists*, not in this house, or anywhere else. I'm sure that there is a perfectly *reasonable* and *scientific* explanation for what just happened here."

"Sure, Mom," Alondra said. "That's just what you said about the piano music, too."

Alondra found a cot in the hall closet and set it up in Mom and Dad's room downstairs. I stood in the doorway and watched.

"Don't you know that a ghost could find you in here, too? It might sit by your bed and watch you sleep."

"Mom, make him *stop!*" Alondra wailed.

"Your sister is right, Dylan, you need to cool it," Mom said. "Now, would you like to sleep downstairs with the rest of us?"

"No. I don't want to sleep down here with the haunted piano."

I smiled and tried to look braver than I felt. Then I turned around and climbed the stairs to the second floor, all alone with the ghosts.

CHAPTER 4

A Rainy Day

"I cannot believe that Uncle Zack only had a *black-and-white* TV," Alondra whined, as we were looking for something to watch the next morning. "And that we only get *three* channels, and there's no cell service out here...or internet..."

"Well, Uncle Zack left a lot of books in the house," Dad said. "Why don't you read a book? It'll pass the time."

Alondra rolled her eyes. "Sure, Dad. If you want to pretend to live in the *nineteenth century.*"

"Alondra, don't be rude to your father," Mom said.

Dad frowned at Alondra and handed us each a plate of toast and eggs. "After we eat, I was thinking that we can spend the day in town," he said. "This rain isn't supposed to let up until tomorrow."

"*What* could we *possibly* do in *this* town?" Alondra moaned.

"Well, I know that your brother is eager to check out the library. And then we can go to the Historical Society. It has a museum with some very good exhibits of local history."

"Such fun," Alondra mumbled.

"*I* like museums," I said.

She scowled at me. "We *know*."

After breakfast, we piled in the car and headed down the road to town. Dad pointed out all the places that he showed me the day we went to the Science Center, but Mom and Alondra weren't impressed.

"So, where's the rest of it?" Alondra asked.

Dad shrugged. "That's it. Well, that, and the harbor."

Alondra sighed and slumped back in her seat, mumbling something that I couldn't hear.

We pulled up in front of the library, which was in an old, white house with a big porch across the front. Dad and I went inside while Mom and Alondra waited for us in the car.

I left Dad looking at the stacks of magazines while I went up to the librarian's desk.

"Excuse me...do you have any books about ghosts?"

The librarian didn't even look up from her computer. "Look in the children's section, fifth row."

I went to the children's section. All that I found there were ghost stories for little kids. The covers had pictures of cartoon ghosts that looked like white sheets, or spooky-looking old houses with bats flying around them.

I went back to the desk. "Excuse me."

"Yes?" The librarian sounded bored.

"I mean...do you have any books about *real* ghosts? Like... what they look like, and how to find them? I, um...think that my house is haunted."

She finally looked at me. "Oh, really?"

"Yeah. We moved into the old house that's next to the lighthouse. My Uncle Zack lived there."

"*Oh!*" She gasped. "So you must be with the new family in town. I *completely* understand, now. Follow me."

I followed the librarian to the other end of the room. "Ah, yes, *here* it is," she said, pulling a book from the shelf. It was big and thick, with a picture of a shadowy-looking man on the cover.

"*Paranormal Investigating?*"

"Yes. I think this book is *exactly* what you need. It may have some unfamiliar words, but I think you can handle it."

Dad and I signed up for our library cards and checked out our books, as sheets of rain spilled off the porch roof like a waterfall. We tried not to get our books wet as we raced to the car, splashing through the puddles in the parking lot. I tripped as I was climbing in the car, and my ghost book flew out of my arms…and into Mom's lap.

"What is *this?*" she asked, picking up my book and wrinkling her nose. "Roger, you know that I don't approve of this weirdo stuff. I can't believe that you allowed Dylan to borrow this. It'll give him nightmares."

"No it won't," I said.

Mom shrugged and gave me back my book. "Fine, young man. When you wake up screaming in the middle of the night, don't come running to us."

"I'm *sure* that Dylan will be *fine* with it, Rorianne," Dad said, as he pulled onto the road and squinted through the downpour.

The town museum was just down the road. Dad pulled up to an old yellow house with an enormous, rusty anchor in the front yard. "This place looks just the same as I remember," he said, smiling. Since the parking lot was empty, he parked right outside the door. "Well, what do you say?" he asked. "Do you want to wait it out, or make a run for it?"

"Make a run for it," Alondra mumbled. "All the way back home. To *New York*."

"That is not what your father meant, and you know that, young lady," Mom said. Alondra sighed, but followed us as we dashed through the rain to the front door.

Inside, an old lady in a long green dress was sitting at a desk, looking through some papers. A little sign on the desk said *Dusty Cooper, Town Historian.*

Dad gasped. *"Mrs. Cooper?"*

The lady stood up and walked over to us. "Roger? Roger Flint?" She peered at Dad's face. "Of *course!* I *thought* I recognized you under that beard! I never forget a face. It's so good to see you after all these years!"

Dad turned to us with a big smile. "This is Mrs. Cooper. She was my high school history teacher!" He looked back at the old lady. "And Mrs. Cooper, *this* is my family." Dad sounded proud as he introduced us all.

As Dad and Mrs. Cooper talked, Mom and I looked at some brochures on the desk while Alondra just stood around looking bored. "...We live in Manhattan now, but we're here for the summer," Dad was saying. "I've been wanting to come back home for years, but...the town isn't the same as I remembered." He looked upset. "What's going on? It's practically deserted. The tourists and summer people should've been here by now. There used to be long lines at the ice cream shop and movie theater, and now they're empty. Half of the houses look abandoned. Even the Science Center is gone."

Mrs. Cooper shook her head. "The town is dying, Roger."

"Dying? But what about the boat building, and the lobster fishing, and the tourists? What *happened?"*

"The tourists just drive through, snap a few pictures of the lighthouse and harbor, then leave. And the Science Center closed years ago, after they lost their funding. Something needs to be done soon, or Salvation Point will be no more."

"Well, this is my town. *I'm* not giving up on it," Dad said. "We hope to come up here every summer from now on. We have a cottage here, now."

"Oh, really?" Mrs. Cooper smiled.

"Yes. We moved into the old light keeper's house out on the point."

Mrs. Cooper's eyes widened. "You can't be serious. *That* place? Roger, you *must* remember the old stories about that house."

Were they the scary stories that Dad was telling us about? I thought. This sounded interesting. I put the pamphlets down and paid attention.

"Sure I remember those stories," Dad said. "But my uncle lived there when I was growing up, and he never had any problems at all. Maybe the ghost got along with him." Dad snickered.

"*Ghost?*" Alondra squealed. She started to turn white.

"What in the *world* are you talking about?" Mom asked. "Is this something that I should know?"

Mrs. Cooper shrugged. "You only moved to the most infamous haunted house in Maine," she said. "Not even those tough, old-time lighthouse keepers would stay there for very long. They would rather lose their jobs than deal with whatever is out there on the point."

Mom frowned. "That's just silly. They must have been *very* superstitious."

"No, they were very stoic, and rational men who were dedicated to their jobs. However, some of them had their wives and children with them, and they didn't want to expose their families to that sort of danger."

"Well, *we* certainly do *not* believe in such things," Mom said.

Maybe you don't, I thought.

Mrs. Cooper just stared at Mom for a second. *"Well!"* she finally said with a smile. I think that she was trying to change the subject. "Given the fact that you're living out there, I *must* show you our lighthouse room first." Mrs. Cooper led us into a room filled with pictures, and glass display cases full of stuff. "This entire room is dedicated to the Salvation Point Light Station, and to the men and women who cared for it throughout its years out on the point."

She pointed to a huge picture hanging beside the door. I recognized our house, but it looked a lot nicer than it did now. "This picture was taken around 1910, during the time that the last permanent lighthouse keeper, Mr. MacMurray, lived there."

"Oh, how beautiful!" Mom said. "Roger, look how pretty it was!"

Mom was right. The house was painted white, with big shutters on the windows. The lawn was mowed and there were nice flowers planted everywhere, a flagpole in the front yard, and a white picket fence near the spot where I found Dad's missing paint.

"Mr. MacMurray kept that lighthouse and property as *neat* as a pin," Mrs. Cooper said. "He took pride in his job, and earned several awards of recognition for his efforts."

"If he could see the place *now*, he'd be rolling in his grave," Mom grumbled.

Dad smiled. "It can look good again, Rorianne. It'll take some time, but we can do it."

Alondra folded her arms and sighed as Mrs. Cooper began talking. "The lighthouse was built in 1842, and the keeper's cottage – your house – was built just a few years later. Life out there was very hard, but simple and good. However, after the untimely death of the last lighthouse keeper, Mr. MacMurray, the U.S. Lighthouse Service – and later, the Coast Guard – had nothing but problems with that place. And *that* is when the ghost stories began, Mrs. Flint."

"I *see*." Mom began to look annoyed at Mrs. Cooper.

"Come here, Mom, look at this stuff," I said. I walked over to a big thing that sat on a rotating platform. "What *is* this?"

"Young man, *that's* the original Fresnel lens from the lighthouse top. It strengthened the light into a beam that could be seen twenty miles out to sea," Mrs. Cooper said. "In the 1960's, the abandoned keeper's cottage was converted into a private home, and the tower was automated. That lens was replaced with a modern, rotating aero-beacon."

I didn't know what an "aero-beacon" was, but that old lighthouse lens was *gigantic!* It reached the *ceiling!* It was shaped like a fat bullet sitting on its end, made of glass slats that sparkled like the crystal chandeliers in the lobby of our apartment building back home. "This thing is *awesome*."

I could tell that Mrs. Cooper was watching me as I looked at the Fresnel lens and the other stuff in the lighthouse room. "I have never seen any other child his age look so interested in the artifacts here," she said to Mom. "When the elementary school students come here on field trips, they all look bored."

Alondra shrugged and gestured at me. "He's a nautical nerd. Like my dad. And don't get him started about sailboats. You'll never shut him up."

"Well, then here is something that might interest you," Mrs. Cooper told me, pointing to an old book lying open under a glass display case. "This is the *Journal of the Light Station*. It's the logbook that belonged to Mr. MacMurray, the lighthouse keeper who lived there at the turn of the century."

I looked down at the book. It was filled up with notes and dates in faded handwriting that was hard to read. It was like a diary of different ships that he saw, and what the weather was like each day. He wrote about getting a shipment of kerosene, and that he painted the railing at the top of the lighthouse.

Meanwhile, Alondra stared at a big black-and-white picture of a skinny man standing in front of the lighthouse. He wore a jacket and tie, and a hat with some kind of emblem on the front. The hat shaded half of his face, but I could still see that he wasn't smiling, and he didn't look very friendly.

Alondra trembled and clutched her chest. I thought that she was going to faint. *"Who is that?"* she whimpered.

"Why, that's Mr. MacMurray, himself."

"That's *him*," Alondra whispered. *"That's* the man...*Mom*...I think I'm gonna be sick. I'm going out to the car."

"Honey, are you ok?" Mom put her arm around her shoulders. Alondra nodded. "I just need to get out of here...*now*."

"I'll take her," Dad said. "You two stay and look at the exhibits."

I wandered around looking at the other things in the lighthouse room, and wondered what Alondra's problem was. The man in that picture looked like a grouch, but there was no reason for her to be scared of him!

"Come on, Dylan, it's time to go," Mom said, not even five minutes after Dad and Alondra went out to the car. I was looking at this big rowboat over in the corner. It was as long as a speedboat, and had a frayed rope draped down along each side. I tried to imagine rowing it in the high waves that crashed up against the rocks...

"Dylan, let's go!" Mom said again. She was getting impatient, as usual. "Your sister is sick, and we need to be getting home."

"But *Mom*," I whined.

"We can come back another time. I'd like to look at those paintings that we passed in the other room. But that's for another day." She dragged me away from the big rowboat and said goodbye to Mrs. Cooper in an unfriendly voice.

"You folks be careful out there at that house," she said.

"*Thank you* for your concern, Mrs. Cooper," Mom said, scowling.

"I hope the young lady will be OK," Mrs. Cooper called as we walked out the door.

On the porch, Mom bent down and looked me in the eye. "Dylan, I don't want you to believe *any* of that nonsense that she told us about our house being haunted. There are no such things as ghosts or haunted houses. Only ignorant people believe in them."

I believed in them, but didn't tell her that as we hurried out to the car. And I thought that *Mrs. Cooper* seemed like a smart lady. It was mean of Mom to say that she was ignorant.

Dad looked surprised when he saw us coming out to the car so soon. "Dad, you should've seen this cool old boat in there," I said as I climbed into the backseat. "The sign under it said that the lighthouse keepers had to row it out and rescue people from shipwrecks -"

"Please, can we talk about something other than that stupid lighthouse?" Alondra snapped.

I turned away from her and started flipping through my library book. "This book is interesting. Listen to this: it says, *'The rarest form of spirit energy is the full-bodied apparition, which can be mistaken for a living human being.'* Maybe that's what you saw in your room, Alondra."

"It *wasn't* a *ghost!*" she cried.

"Dylan, you're not helping the situation," Dad mumbled.

Mom scowled at me. "Dylan, that's *enough!* I see that that book of yours is going to put crazy ideas into your head. You're already beginning to exasperate me."

I shrugged and looked out the window as we headed down the dirt road toward home.

"Dylan, look at that freighter out in the bay," Dad said, pointing at the ocean. I could see just a big gray shape, covered with lights that barely cut through the rain and fog. "It must be anchored there because of the weather."

"Who cares," Alondra mumbled.

Dad smirked. "I bet *you'll* care in just a second. You'll see." He pulled up to the house and we were heading inside when –

HONNNNNK! We all jumped and Alondra shrieked.

"*What* was *that?*" Mom cried.

"It's just the ship. I told you -"

"So you mean that we have to listen to that thing *all night?*" Alondra wailed.

"It's no worse than the honking horns and traffic that you hear every day back home."

"That's different. I'd give *anything* to go home right now." Alondra burst out crying, and ran inside.

"She can't be feeling too sick," Mom said, watching as Alondra stomped up the stairs. Her door slammed a second later.

I headed up to my room and stretched out on my bed with the ghost book, listening to the ship honking in the bay, and the rain tapping on the roof. I thought about how the librarian and the cops had hinted that there was something strange going on at our house. Mrs. Cooper even said that it was haunted. I wondered if I could solve the mystery of our house before we had to go back home to the city.

CHAPTER 5

Matthias

J wasn't sure what woke me up that night. It could've been the icy cold air that filled my room, even though a warm breeze blew through the open window. It could've been the sound of someone turning pages in a book, which I could still hear over the dripping rain outside. Maybe it was the foghorn honking on that ship that was anchored in the bay. Or maybe it was the deep man's voice that I heard somewhere nearby.

"Well, well. *This* gives me an idea," the voice said. It sounded like a page turned again.

What was Dad doing in here in the middle of the night? I wondered. *Why is he reading in the dark and talking to himself?*

"Hmm. Fascinating."

Another page turned.

"*Dad?*"

The lighthouse beam flashed into my window and traveled across the walls, falling for a moment on a person standing across the room. It wasn't Dad. I took a deep breath and turned on the light next to my bed.

A tall, brown-haired man was standing beside the desk, flipping through the ghost book. He wore a necktie, and a blue coat with fancy patches on the collar and two rows of buttons down the front, like an old sea captain.

I gasped and pulled my blankets up under my chin as the man turned and smiled at me. "I am so glad to find some new books here!" he said. "I have had the same reading material for decades."

I just stared at him, too afraid to move, or call for Mom and Dad. Was this the guy that Alondra saw in her room? Was he a burglar? What did he *want*?

"Excuse me a moment." He set the library book down and walked through the wall.

My mouth dropped open as I stared at the spot where the man had disappeared. I couldn't believe it. He had just walked...through...the *wall!* I gulped and pulled my blankets over my head. He wasn't a burglar at all. He was a *ghost!*

When I heard my door open, I peeked out of my blankets and watched as he came back in. He was holding the thick book that Dad had been reading. "See?" he said. "I found *this* book as well. A novel!"

I froze and squeezed my eyes shut, hoping that he'd go away. Maybe when I opened them, the man would be gone and I'd be alone again...

I opened my eyes, only to find him watching me, still holding Dad's book. This time I tried not to panic, and just studied him. He wasn't glowing. I couldn't see through him. He looked...ordinary, and he didn't seem to want to hurt me.

And he couldn't have been that bad, if it only took a couple of books to make him happy.

The man...*ghost*...walked over and stood next to my bed. He began reading the back of Dad's book. "This tells the story of a detective who must solve a series of *lurid* and *ghastly* murders. It sounds very exciting!" He tucked the book under his arm and wandered over to the dresser, where he picked up the old binoculars. "My mother bought me these binoculars when I began my employment here," he said as he looked them over. "They were very expensive, one of the best made. I gently scolded Mother for purchasing such an extravagant gift, for she was certainly not a wealthy woman."

He set the book and binoculars back on the dresser and looked at me. "I have been observing your family for the past few days. You are...*Dylan*, I believe?"

I nodded. "Who...who *are* you? A sea captain?"

The man snorted. "A *sea captain?* Do I look like a *sea captain* to you?"

"Y...y...yes, sir."

"Well, listen up, child. I'm not a sea captain; I'm the keeper of this lighthouse. MacMurray's the name. Matthias MacMurray." He thrust out his big right hand, and I backed up against the wall without taking my eyes off his face. I really didn't want to touch a ghost.

"What's the matter, sonny? Do you fear that my condition is contagious? Or is it that your mother never taught you to greet your elders?"

He continued to look at me, holding out his hand. I gulped again, reached out, and shook it. His hand was cold, but it felt as solid as my own. That made me feel a little better.

"Uh...Mr. MacMurray -"

"*Matthias, please!* None of this *Mr. MacMurray* nonsense."

"Um... Matthias? You...you live in my *room?*"

"*Your* room?" He looked surprised. "This is *my* room, sonny. Been that way for over a hundred years. But I suppose there's nothing I can do about it now." He shrugged. "Looks like we're roommates."

That's what you think, I thought. *I* wasn't going to share my room with a grumpy old ghost. I wondered if Mom and Dad would switch rooms with me. Alondra wouldn't, just to be mean to me...no matter how much she hated those creepy portraits.

"Matthias? You, um...really lived here for a hundred years?"

He sat down in the big chair in the corner, sighed, and ran his fingers through his hair. He didn't have his lighthouse keeper's hat on, like he had in that picture at the museum. "Actually, one hundred and twenty-five. But let me tell you a story, sonny. It all started the night of the storm. It was the winter of 1913 when a nor'easter blew in; it was the worst storm in years. Long story short, the whole lighthouse top was covered with ice. I had to go outside the lantern room to repair a windowpane that had broken during the storm. A big gust of wind came up, and I slipped on the ice and fell beneath the railing to the rocks below. I lost my hat during my plunge to the ground, but felt no pain upon landing. I just remembered watching as some of the townsfolk discovered my body the next day. I witnessed my own funeral, and learned that my distraught mother had purchased a nice headstone for my grave. I attempted to comfort her in her grief, but alas, she could not see or hear me."

Matthias scowled at the floor and shook his head. "I knew that it was my own carelessness that resulted in that accident, which allowed the lamp to burn out on a night when it was needed the most."

"But you couldn't help that! You, um..."

"*Died*? You can say the word. But after that, I vowed that I would stay here and never allow the light to go out again!

"A new keeper was immediately appointed to take my place, and I observed his work with the *utmost* criticism. However, he wasn't doing the job to my satisfaction, so I chased him off. They hired others, one right after the other. I was not pleased with their work, either, and I let them know! Every man fled the place in terror, and so they were immediately dismissed from employment. They were told that it was disgraceful of them to abandon their posts in such a cowardly manner."

I wondered why all those grown-up men had been so afraid of Matthias that they would run away and lose their jobs. Matthias looked just like a living person. I realized that he wasn't scary, at all.

He went to the window and looked out at the lighthouse, nodded once, and sat back down in his chair. "There was one fellow who boasted that he did not believe in ghosts, and he teased and taunted me to come out and show myself. However, he lasted only a week. He claimed that I tried to push him down the lighthouse stairs, and that he was physically as-saulted by an...ahem...*invisible entity*. He *feared* for his *life*!" Matthias snickered.

"After a while, the Lighthouse Service couldn't find a single keeper who would stay here overnight. They could not figure out why the lamp came on by itself every night, without *living* hands to tend it. Oh, they made inquiries, and had inspectors come out to find out what was going on, but there was nothing wrong with *my* light. *No*, sir, not on *my* watch! Finally, they just boarded up the house, and I had it all to myself again. Just the way I liked it."

"But didn't you ever want someone to stay here and help you? And, you know, have someone to talk to?"

"I didn't need any help! And I was too busy with my duties to bother with people. Besides, I had plenty of visitors. As the years went by, the young people in town started saying that this place was haunted. They would come *snooping* around with their cameras, trying to take my picture and make contact with me. *Fools! I* didn't give 'em what they wanted. Soon, they would get bored and leave me alone, but with each new generation, it starts up again.

"Then, along came your uncle. He bought the place cheap, since no one else wanted it. The house had been abandoned for years. Now, *he* was a good tenant. He didn't bother me or mess with the lighthouse, so I never bothered him. And his presence kept those blasted ghost hunters away. So did his hives of bees. But now that I'm playing host to a family of landlubbers -"

"We're *not* landlubbers! My dad's a sailor. A *real* sailor. He's taken me sailing out on the Hudson River since I was three years old! He taught me how to be a sailor, too, and he built me my own boat when I turned ten."

"A *sailor?* A little slip of a boy like you?" Matthias looked startled. "Well, then you be careful out there, sonny. Stay away from these cliffs; they're dangerous. That's why the lighthouse is here."

He stood up and looked out at the lighthouse again, then back at me. "Go to sleep, now. I'll be very busy tonight. It could be bad for the mariners out there in this fog."

The ghost vanished without another word, and my room grew warm again.

Did he really expect me to sleep tonight? I wondered. He had seemed nice enough to me, but I felt nervous knowing that he had attacked that man. I laid awake for a long time, wondering if he would become my friend, or if he would chase us away like he did to all those men back in 1913.

CHAPTER 6

The Haunted Lighthouse

"Well, it's about time you got up!" Mom said, smiling, as I trudged down the stairs the next morning. Dad and Alondra were already in the kitchen, helping Mom as she made breakfast. "Did you sleep well?"

"No. The ghost of the lighthouse keeper talked to me last night."

Mom frowned at me. "Dylan, stop being silly. There's no such thing as ghosts."

I jumped, startled, as Matthias appeared behind Mom. He was looking at the bowl of pancake batter and the electric egg-beater that she had set down on the counter.

"But there *is* a ghost, Mom! It's a man; his name's Matthias. And he's standing right behind you!"

Alondra rolled her eyes. "Oh, grow *up!*"

"Hey, hold on a minute Rorianne...you too, Alondra," Dad said. "This is an old house; a lot has happened here. And a man did die out at the lighthouse, years ago."

Matthias picked up the electric eggbeater and looked at it with a frown, turning it this way and that. *Why* couldn't the others *see* him?

"Roger, please. People die everywhere. And you shouldn't encourage our son to make up stories about things that don't exist."

"But *Mom!*"

She held up her hand. "Enough. I don't want to hear any more talk about ghosts. And that goes for you too, Roger."

Matthias disappeared, along with the eggbeater.

Mom turned back to the counter and gasped. "*What* in the world...what happened to my *mixer?* I was just *using* it!"

I laughed. Maybe she would believe me, *now*.

"This is not funny, young man!" Mom cried, pointing at me with her mixing spoon. But that only made me laugh harder.

Mom found her missing eggbeater sitting on the couch that afternoon. Dried pancake batter was splattered on the wall and smeared into the couch cushions. Mom said that it was a mystery how it ended up there, but she made *me* clean up the mess.

Having Matthias around might not be so much fun, after all.

***

Later that night, I was almost asleep when I heard footsteps on the creaking floor behind me. Then it sounded like someone was rummaging through the desk drawers, and mumbling to themselves.

I looked over at the dark shape of Matthias bending over the desk, and then I squinted at the clock on my nightstand.

"It's *eleven o'clock*," I said. "What are you *doing?*"

"It's time to trim the wicks, m'boy. Gotta do it every night."

"Every *night?* Why?"

"To keep the flame burning brightly. And to prevent smoke from leaving soot on the lamp." He walked over and stood next to my bed. "Would you like to come with me and see how I do it?"

I groaned. "Go to sleep. You don't need to do that stuff anymore. Dad said that the light comes on by itself, now. Some man just comes by to check it sometimes."

Matthias put his hands on his hips and glared down at me. "*I am responsible for this light station, sonny!* When it's time to trim the wicks, I *trim the wicks!* If I shirk my duties, the sailors could *die!* And then it would be my fault for not tending the light. Why can't you understand that, boy?"

But you're dead, I thought. *And they don't even use wicks anymore.* I wanted to tell him that, but kept quiet. Matthias had turned away and stood looking out my window with his hands behind his back. He seemed to be remembering something.

He finally turned and looked at me. "I have work to do," he mumbled. "I will return later." He walked through the wall and I heard him thumping around downstairs, until the house grew quiet and I went back to sleep.

***

I didn't see Matthias when I got up the next morning. Maybe he was mad at me because I didn't go watch him trim the wicks last night.

I figured that he was still around, though. When I went to the kitchen to get some cereal, a cabinet door opened and closed by itself. Then I heard a long slurping sound behind me, and Mom's steaming mug of coffee hovered in mid-air.

I ignored the floating coffee mug and sat down to eat. Matthias burped as the empty mug settled back onto the table.

Weird. I didn't know that ghosts could drink. So where did the coffee go? I would have to ask Matthias how that worked.

I shivered and rubbed my arms as I ate my cereal. It was *cold* in here. I think Matthias made it that way. But it was already hot outside, and a warm breeze blew through the window screens. The ocean washed up on the rocks, and the wind chime rattled on the porch. It was the perfect weather to go sailing. I wondered if Dad would let me.

Mom shuffled into the kitchen, shivering. "There are *always* such *drafts* in this house. And you never know *where* they might be." She sat down in Matthias's chair and stared at her empty coffee mug. "What on *earth?* I'm positive that I just filled this five minutes ago." She sighed and took the cup over to the counter.

"Dylan, did you drink my coffee? And don't lie to me, young man!"

"No, Mom, I didn't drink your coffee. I hate coffee. Matthias drank it."

"*Matthias,*" Mom grumbled. "Look, it doesn't matter that you drank the coffee, Dylan. I don't care about that. What matters is it that you just lied about it."

"But I didn't *drink* it, Mom! You have to *believe* me!"

"Umm-hmmm…" She just turned around and glared at me. "And I don't suppose that you've seen my *dish towel*, have you? I had it right here on the counter."

"No, I didn't see your dish towel. Why would I want to take your dish towel?" I got up and put my cereal dish in the sink. "Can I go outside?"

"Only if you stay out of trouble. Stay in the yard, and don't go near the water. And while you're out there, you need to think about all this lying that you've been doing. Come back in when you're ready to apologize and tell me the truth."

I didn't argue with her. If I did, she'd send me to my room.

As I escaped outside, Dad wandered into the living room, scratching his head and looking around, puzzled. "Has anyone seen my book?" he asked Mom. "I just had it the other night..."

Matthias appeared beside me as I hopped off the porch and into the front yard. "That coffee hit the spot," he said, smiling and patting his stomach. "And it's going to be a fine day."

I looked up at him as I followed him across the yard, the dewy grass soaking my sneakers. "Aren't you hot in that jacket? It's already seventy-five degrees out here."

"I don't feel a thing."

I was ready to ask him about the coffee when I noticed something shiny lying beneath Alondra's window. "What's all this?" I knelt in the tall grass and picked up some tubes of lipstick and containers of other makeup, and bottles of nail polish. I even found a fancy little glass bottle of perfume. "This is Alondra's stuff! *You...you threw* it out the *window!* Yeah...it must've been the other night, when she saw you in her room!"

Matthias didn't look at me. He just stared straight ahead and stalked toward the lighthouse as I trotted along behind him.

"I didn't mean to frighten the young lady," he grumbled. "However, when I saw that feminine paraphernalia on her dresser, I was *scandalized*, and I...I *disapproved!* I will not permit such rubbish in this house!"

"Why? What's wrong with Alondra's makeup?"

"You mean that...that *face paint?*" He looked disgusted. "*Respectable* women do not paint their faces or wear trousers, like your mother and sister do!"

"Don't be dumb. Girls can wear whatever they want now."

"And that unseemly photograph of that *immodestly* dressed young man that she pinned up over one of the portraits..." Matthias shuddered. "Why does your father allow such a thing?"

"What do you mean? That's just a poster of her favorite singer."

Matthias just grunted. "Humph. Highly inappropriate. Back in *my* day, men dressed like *gentlemen*, and women were *ladies*." He reached out and plucked something out of my hand. "However, I was quite puzzled about this tiny bottle of paint. It is too small to be of practical use." He held up a bottle of sparkly blue nail polish, and peered at it in the sunlight.

"Never mind that. You better put *all* of this *back* in her room *tonight!* Everyone keeps blaming *me* for the stuff that you do!" I shoved the rest of the makeup into his hands and glared at him.

He looked at me, surprised, and slowly stuffed it all into his pockets. Then he mumbled something under his breath and didn't say another word about Alondra and her makeup.

He sure was in a crabby mood that morning.

When we reached the lighthouse, Matthias blocked the door and looked down at me with his arms folded. "I observed you all when you arrived here. You appeared to be a nice family."

"We *are* a nice family. Well, except for *Alondra*." I shrugged. "Matthias? Why didn't you just show up and talk to us when we moved in? Why did you play the piano and knock on the walls and scare us?"

"That's just a typical haunting. I wished to see how you and your family would react to my presence. I tried to welcome you all with some fine classical music on the piano, and I even left a flower on the table for the lady. However, she doesn't even believe that I exist!" Matthias scowled. "You and your father seemed to accept me. But that sister of yours is something else. And your mother seems like a most difficult woman to live with. I was *furious* when the ladies took those portraits down from the bedroom walls!"

"Did you paint them, Matthias?"

"No. Your uncle hung them there when your dad was a boy. But they became a part of *my* house, and I *don't* want them removed!"

We went in the little building that was attached to the bottom of the lighthouse. Dad was fixing it up it into an art studio for Mom.

"This is another thing!" Matthias snapped, gesturing at the wet paintings leaning against the walls. "This is my work room. Now, how am I supposed to work in here? I cannot perform my duties with these *paintings* scattered about!"

"Those are my mom's paintings. And you better not touch them. She gets mad at us if we do."

"Then she better not leave them on the floor. They're in my way."

I was all out of breath by the time we reached the top of the lighthouse. Halfway up, I had wanted to stop and rest, but didn't want Matthias to think I was a wimp. He jogged up the steep, winding stairs as I puffed and panted behind him. It was no wonder he was so skinny. He must've been in great shape.

"Ah, that gets the old heart a-pumping!" he said with a grin, as I plodded up the steps. "However, you look winded. Let us step out to the gallery so you may catch your breath." He opened the door to the balcony at the lighthouse top.

"Don't you mean the balcony?" I asked.

"No, I mean the *gallery*."

We stood at the railing and watched as an old-time schooner sailed out of the harbor and headed for the lighthouse. "Isn't she a beauty?" Matthias said, pointing at the ship. "They just don't build vessels like that anymore."

"Yeah. I hope *I* can buy a boat like that someday. I would live on it and sail it all over the world! You and Dad could come with me and be my crew."

Matthias stared at me for a moment. "You know, sonny, you remind me of your father when he was a boy. The resemblance is uncanny. He was quiet, but curious, like you. He was always exploring everything, like the time when you were meddling in the storeroom and playing with my binoculars."

"You knew my dad? Before we moved here, I mean?"

Matthias nodded. "Many years ago, I watched your father every time he would come to visit Zachary. Your father was no older than you are, now. I saw him grow up, and realized how much he loved this light station. Your uncle made a wise choice in leaving the property to your father. Who knows what would have become of it?" He looked up at the lantern room windows and nodded at me. "We should continue on, now. There is work to be done."

Matthias floated through the door to the lantern room, and unlocked it for me to follow him. I stepped inside and looked around –

"WATCH IT, WATCH IT!" Matthias panicked and pushed me against the windows. "You have to be *careful* up here! You almost bumped into the *lens!* It is very expensive, and those prisms are too easy to scratch and chip."

I stared at him. "The lens?"

"Yes. This is a first-order Fresnel lens. That is the largest and most powerful lighthouse lens made." His panicked expression softened as he smiled, and looked up at the middle of the room. "Isn't it beautiful?"

I didn't see anything except the modern light, which looked like a big drum mounted sideways on a metal stand. I didn't tell Matthias that, though. I realized that the ghost could still see things from back in his time, even though they were gone now. But to be polite, I agreed that the Fresnel lens was beautiful.

Matthias looked pleased. "I dust and polish it every morning," he said, as a soft cloth appeared in his hand. He ignored the modern light and began making wiping motions in mid-air. He sure looked funny, waving the cloth above his head as he dusted the old-time lens that I couldn't see. "Of course, back in my day, I had to wear a soft linen smock to prevent my coat buttons from scratching the lens. However, in my ghostly state, that is no longer necessary." He looked down at me with a big grin. "And now you can be my assistant! You can wash the windows!"

I looked down when I felt something bump against my legs. A bucket had appeared beside me, filled to the top with water. Mom's missing dish towel hung over the side.

Matthias handed me a roll of paper towels from the kitchen. It was strange that I hadn't seen him carrying it up here. "Make sure that you dry the windows well, so it doesn't leave water spots."

I hated helping Mom clean the cottage, but helping Matthias in the lighthouse was fun. Matthias didn't say much as he worked, so I started to pretend that I lived here back in his time and I really was his assistant, doing this every day.

"Matthias?" I finally said. "You sounded so...so...*mad* at us before. You were complaining about everything, like you wanted us to leave. But now you, I don't know, seem really happy..."

He nodded. "And you're wondering why, aren't you? Well, that's because coming up here *makes* me happy. When I'm here at the top of the lighthouse, nothing else seems important. Look out those windows, boy. We live in the prettiest place around. How can you look at all that and not feel happy?

"This place gets in your blood," he continued, as he dusted the lens and I washed the windows. "It gets a hold of you and never lets go. I suppose that if I have to be stuck on earth, this is a fine place to stay."

I wanted to hang out with Matthias all day, but when I heard footsteps on the stairs, I knew that wasn't going to happen. Voices echoed below us and grew louder, as Mom, Dad, and even...*Alondra* headed to the lighthouse top.

"Listen, I think he's in the lantern room," Dad said. "He knows that's off limits."

I frowned and scrubbed at some grime on the windowsill, ignoring everyone when they appeared at the door.

"*There* you are!" Mom said. "We were looking *all over* for you, young man!"

Dad cleared his throat. "Dylan, how did you get in here? The door to the lantern room is supposed to be kept closed and locked at all times."

"Matthias let me in." I continued washing the windows as Mom and Dad looked at each other. They looked stunned.

Alondra smirked. "Oh, look at Dylan, pretending to be a lighthouse keeper. How cute." I stuck my tongue out at her when Mom and Dad weren't looking. Matthias frowned at me and shook his head.

"Dylan, you shouldn't be up here by yourself; those stairs could be dangerous," Dad said. "And I told you that none of us are allowed to be in here. This is expensive equipment. If it's damaged, we could be in trouble."

"But it's *our* lighthouse!"

"And that's *my* dish towel!" Mom pulled it right out of my hands and stuck it in my face. "You told me that you didn't take it, and here it is!"

"But I didn't *take* it, Mom, I swear! It was Matthias!"

"Dylan, you've already lied to me. Don't you *dare* try to blame some imaginary dead man. You'll only make it worse for yourself."

"But *Mom!*" I looked around for Matthias, wondering what he thought about all this. He had disappeared, but I noticed his dust cloth still waving around in the air above our heads. I hoped that nobody would look up and see it.

"Hey, look at that bird!" I said, pointing outside to where a seagull sat perched on the railing.

"That's just a stupid seagull!" Alondra snapped. But everyone watched as it flew away, and never saw Matthias's cloth.

"Dylan, we came up here to tell you to go get your swimsuit and get in the car," Mom said. "We're going to the pool for the day, and getting pizza later."

"But I don't want to go to the pool. I want to stay here."

Mom scowled at me. "You know that you can't stay home without adult supervision."

"Matthias is an adult; he can supervise me."

"Don't be funny. Now, just this morning, you have lied *twice*, and you've gone into the lantern room when you *know* that it's forbidden. You are on *thin ice*, mister."

"But I wasn't being funny..."

Matthias appeared again, holding his cloth in both hands and watching us.

"Mom, I thought that you wanted me to make *friends!* And Matthias is my friend. He's showing me around the lighthouse. I *promise* I'll do what he says, and I won't get in any trouble!"

Mom folded her arms. "*Matthias,* hmmm? Look around, Dylan; there is *nobody* up here but us. So tell me, what does *Matthias* look like?"

I shrugged. "I dunno. Just a man."

Alondra snickered. "That's *it?* You mean that he doesn't look like a white sheet?"

"You're so dumb!"

"Dylan, don't call your sister names," Dad said in a low voice. "Now, go get your stuff. We'll be waiting for you in the car." Dad picked up my bucket and paper towels, and we headed for the stairs.

I looked back into the lantern room and gasped. For a second – just a second – I saw the big Fresnel lens sparkling in the sunlight as Matthias polished every piece of its glass. But when I blinked, it was gone.

I sighed. "See you later, Matthias."

He nodded. "I'll be here. When I'm through with this, I have to disassemble and clean the lamp."

I knew that the lamp was gone now, too.

***

Pizza and swimming would've been a *perfect* day back home in the city. But now that I met Matthias, I didn't care about that stuff. Spending time with him was a lot more interesting than a day at a pool. I might not always have the chance to talk with a real ghost.

But I had to go to the pool with everyone, anyway. It was boring. I swam a little, even though Mom kept calling me back and telling me not to go toward the deep end. Then she kept pointing out other boys my age, and telling me to go over and introduce myself. I wished that she would leave me alone.

On the way home, we stopped at Pies on the Point, the pizza place across from the cemetery. "Mom, I want to go look around in that graveyard," I said.

Mom frowned. "Dylan, *why* would you want to look at something like *that?*"

"Because he's *weird*, Mom, I *told* you that," Alondra said.

"Okay," Mom said, looking at her watch. "But hurry up. The pizzas won't take long to bake, and then we're taking them home."

I turned and ran through the iron gate before she could change her mind. In the distance, I could just see the top of the lighthouse over the trees.

I hadn't planned on visiting the graveyard, but now that I was there, I knew what I had to do. I walked over the short grass, past rows of shiny white gravestones with flowers planted around them. It was like *something* – I don't know what - was leading me to a section in the back, under some shady trees. The grass was higher back there, the graves older and faded. Grasshoppers leaped out of my way as I parted the tall grass that tickled my bare legs. I turned left at a dead stump, then right at a prickly bush that hid a row of little stones underneath it...and there it was. A worn-out gravestone poked up out of the weeds. Moss filled in some of the letters that read:

Matthias MacMurray
1868 – 1913
Beloved Son

Underneath were the letters *U.S.L.H.S.* I knew that they stood for *United States Lighthouse Service*.

"It's really true," I whispered.

I jumped up and ran halfway to the car. "*Mom!* Mom, come here!" I called. "I found Matthias's grave! Maybe you'll believe me, *now*."

"We don't have *time* for that, Dylan. I don't need to see an old grave. If we stay here, the pizzas will get cold."

I glared at her. "Dad hasn't even come *out* with the pizzas yet!" I turned around and stomped back into the cemetery, ignoring Mom as she ordered me to get in the car.

I knelt down and peeled the moss off Matthias's gravestone, trying not to think about his skeleton buried below me. *That* was too creepy. The *real* Matthias – the Matthias I knew – was still around and working at the lighthouse, one hundred years after he died.

I pulled out some tall weeds around the bottom of the stone, and stepped back to look at it. Matthias's grave looked kind of lonely, sitting off by itself. It was like people had forgotten about him. I picked a flower and set it on top of the stone...and then spun around when I heard someone swishing through the tall grass behind me.

It was only Dad. I should've known that Mom wouldn't walk back there.

"Young man, you need to come back to the car immediately," Dad rumbled. I knew that he was mad when he talked really quiet like that. "Your mother told me that you mouthed off to her, and wouldn't do what she said. She is very upset with you right now."

"Well, *I'm* upset with *her*. She never listens to *anything* I say. She just thinks I'm *lying* to her, and I'm *not!*"

"I know, Dylan. Believe me, I know."

"She wouldn't even come and see Matthias's grave. I bet she's afraid to see proof that he's real."

Dad stared down at the stone as if he was thinking about something. I was surprised when he picked another flower and laid it alongside mine. "Now, come on. We need to get home."

I could tell that Mom was really mad at me, because she didn't talk to me until we got home. When we did, she just handed me a glass of milk and plate of pizza, and pointed up the stairs. "Dylan, take your dinner and go up to your room."

Alondra smirked. "Yeah, go on upstairs with the ghost man that you like so much."

"Alondra, don't ridicule your brother, or you'll be joining him!" Dad said.

Mom and Dad had rented a movie that I really wanted to see. As I slumped on my bed and picked at my pizza, I could hear everyone downstairs laughing and talking about the characters. I remembered how Mom wouldn't listen to me when I told her about Matthias. The longer that I thought about her, the madder I got.

I even ignored Matthias when he appeared next to me. If he knew why I was sent to my room, he would tell me to obey my parents. I wasn't in the mood for a lecture.

Instead, he told me that I did a good job on the windows, and that I would make a fine Assistant Keeper. "...And I understand that you explored the cemetery this afternoon," he continued. "I saw you from the lighthouse top, and watched you through my binoculars. Thanks for the flower."

I shrugged. "It's no big deal. Dad left you one, too."

"So...why are you up here by yourself, sonny? Everyone is downstairs watching a humorous moving picture. Haven't you been wanting to see it?"

I grinned. I couldn't help it. I thought it was funny that Matthias called movies *moving pictures*, but I didn't want to tell him what happened. "I don't want to talk about it," I mumbled.

"I see." He pointed at my plate. "What is that you're eating?"

"It's pizza. You never had pizza?"

He shook his head. "May I have a taste?"

"You mean, you can *eat?*"

"I can drink coffee, can't I?"

Yeah, and it got me into trouble, I thought. But I broke off a piece of pizza and handed it to him, gawking at him as he ate it. If he disappeared, wouldn't the chewed-up pizza land on the floor?

Matthias went to the window and looked out at the lighthouse, his back to me. Slowly, I reached for my camera that was sitting on my nightstand. I turned it on and aimed it at him...

Matthias didn't even turn around. "Dylan, I trust you, that you will not try to photograph me as if I am a curiosity."

"But I just want to take a picture of you to show Mom."

"Absolutely not." He held out his hand. "Give me the camera."

"Don't throw it out the window!" I begged as I handed it to him. "I just got it for Christmas."

The camera disappeared as soon as he touched it. I gasped. "Where'd it go?"

"It's in safekeeping until you forget this *entire* idea."

"But you can't just take our stuff!" I wailed. Matthias scowled at me and disappeared.

Later, I found my camera sitting on the dresser. I didn't know where Matthias was, so I snatched it up and looked it over. It wasn't broken.

I didn't want Matthias to get mad and not talk to me anymore, so I never tried to take his picture again. He said that he trusted me. I didn't want to let him down.

CHAPTER 7

Summer

$\mathcal{J}$uly went by fast, and I tried to forget that we would have to go home in just one more month. This was the best summer *ever*, and I didn't want it to end! Every day at low tide, I climbed down the cliff to see if any new shells and sea glass had washed up on the rocks. Sometimes I searched the yard with the metal detector, but never found a trace of Captain Cutlass's treasure.

On rainy days, Dad took me to the library to get new books. Sometimes we rented movies and had pizza from Pies on the Point. Dad was right: they *did* make the best pizza that I ever tasted.

I took *Thunder* out sailing every chance I could, and I only tipped over *twice* in the whole month! Dad showed me how to pull the boat back upright, though, so it wasn't a big deal. He said that I was getting better every day, and maybe soon I'd be good enough to enter a *race!* I knew that Salvation Point held sailboat races – *regattas*, Dad called them – for kids my age. I got excited about that, until Mom reminded us that we would be going home soon. I knew that she and Alondra couldn't wait to leave.

Alondra had a calendar in her room where she marked off the days until we moved back home. Still, she didn't complain as much, anymore. She had met some lifeguard at the pool, and she wouldn't stop talking about how *cuuuute* he was. Now she always wanted to go to the pool just so she could see him. I will never understand her.

One day, Dad built a stone fireplace in the backyard. We had the *best* campfires! At night we all sat by the fire, watching the flames and looking at the stars. Dad pointed out constellations that we couldn't see back in the city, since the sky was so bright there. As it got later at night, the lights across the bay would go out, one by one, and I knew it was time to go to bed. We had to use flashlights when we went back to the house. Even with the moonlight and the lighthouse, it was *dark* here!

Sometimes, I spotted Matthias standing in the shadows and watching us as we talked and told stories by the campfire. I always waved him over to join us, but he would just smile at me and disappear. I knew that he had gone to stand his watch in the lighthouse.

I could never get Matthias to understand that he didn't have to work in the lighthouse anymore. I gave up after a few days. Instead, I started following him around as he did his chores. I helped him sweep the stairs, and watch for ships. He didn't tell me *why* we had to watch for ships; we just did. I even snuck outside one night to watch him trim the wicks. Matthias seemed proud of the lighthouse, as he explained what he was doing and showed me how all the invisible equipment worked.

"...Now, look at *this*, sonny," Matthias said when we were working at the lighthouse top one day. I tried to pay attention as he pointed to something that wasn't there anymore. "During the night, this weight that you see here slowly descends on this cable, all the way to the bottom of the tower, and turns these clockwork gears over here. Those gears are what make the lens revolve. Then every four hours, we must crank the weight back to the top so it may begin its descent once more. Do you understand?"

I'd understand it more if I could see it, I thought. But I just nodded as Matthias smiled and moved on to the next piece of missing machinery.

Really, I never spotted the Fresnel lens again, or saw the wicks or kerosene lamp. I had no idea what that weight and gears looked like. But I pretended that I could see everything, so I wouldn't hurt his feelings.

On the Fourth of July, Dad took us to a parade and carnival in the next town. It was fun, even though Mom wouldn't let me go on the grown-up rides with Dad and Alondra. Dad gave me some money to spend any way I wanted. I wasted most of it at a game where I tried to win a goldfish. Then Dad talked me into playing another game where I won a little stuffed alien, instead. Later, Dad took me into a big barn where we could pet some farm animals. Mom and Alondra said the animals stunk, so they stayed outside.

That night, we sat by the cliff to watch the town fireworks. The fire department set them off from a barge out in the harbor. Matthias sat down next to me, folding his legs up under himself like a kid. "Isn't this magnificent?" he kept saying. "Oh, oh, look at *that* one! What a *grand* display! I tell you, sonny, they get better *every* year, and I have witnessed over a *century* of Independence Days!"

Matthias was usually so *serious*. I was glad that he joined us to watch the fireworks.

***

As the weeks went by, the spooky things that Matthias did were starting to seem...well, *normal*. I got used to seeing him appear when I didn't expect him. Sometimes he turned the TV or radio on in the middle of the night. But when something went missing, I didn't worry about it anymore. I knew that he had just taken it to look at and would bring it back.

Matthias could be annoying, though. I woke up one night to the sound of piano keys clinking downstairs. First one note, then another, like a little kid was trying it out. I groaned. What was Matthias up to, *now?*

I crept downstairs and peeked around the corner. The full moon shown through the curtains, lighting the living room enough for me to see him sitting at the piano, plunking on the keys with one finger. He looked at me. "What are you doing?" I whispered. "You're gonna wake everybody up!"

"It's my habit to play the piano by the light of the full moon. I just cannot suppress my ghostly routines!" He started pounding on the keys. "This is the Fifth Symphony, of Beethoven!" he cried. "A *fine* composer!"

"I don't *care* who wrote it!" I shouted over the music. "You're going to get me in *trouble!*"

"Yes, you *are* in trouble, young man!" Mom snapped, as she and Dad stormed into the living room. "It's twelve-o-clock at night! You're down here playing the piano at *midnight?*"

"But Mom, it wasn't *me!* It was -"

She held up her hand. *"Don't* say it, Dylan. I've had it up to *here* with this ghost nonsense. It's really exasperating me!"

Matthias kept looking from Mom and Dad, back to me. He looked sorry that he'd gotten me in trouble. He picked up his ragged old music book and tossed it at Mom's feet. It landed with a fluttering of pages that opened at *Beethoven's Fifth Symphony*.

Mom gasped and covered her mouth, staring down at the book. "Dylan," she said. "How...did you just...do that?" Then she shook her head and straightened up, like she was trying not to believe what she just saw. "It's time for you to go to sleep. I don't want to hear any more noise out here."

"But Mom -"

"Dylan, you heard your mother. I don't know what was *really* going on out here, but you need to go back to bed before you wake up your sister," Dad said.

As they headed back to their room, I heard Mom gasp again. "*Roger?* I just thought of something. When did *Dylan* learn to play the piano?"

Dad shrugged. "Never. Maybe he's telling you the truth, Rorianne..."

Matthias had disappeared, but as I headed back upstairs, I hoped he wouldn't follow me to my room and bother me. I was mad at him for playing the piano after I told him not to, and then getting me in trouble with Mom. I didn't want to talk to him for the rest of the night.

***

Almost every day, tourists pulled into our driveway to take pictures of the lighthouse. Artists set up easels to paint pictures of it. Sometimes, Dad would unlock it so people could climb to the top. They *oohed* and *ahhed* over the view and took pictures of each other standing by the railing. Matthias always followed them around the lighthouse top and watched them with a frown.

The hot, sunny days were the busiest ones for the tourists. One hot day, Dad started to paint the house while Mom and Alondra laid outside in their swimsuits to work on their tans. But as carloads of people filled the driveway and wandered around the lighthouse, Mom and Alondra decided to stop sunbathing, and Dad put away his paint.

"Roger, this is getting ridiculous," Mom complained. "We shouldn't allow all these strangers to go trampling over our property."

"Give 'em a break, Rorianne; they're on vacation. They just want to look at the lighthouse. And if I remember correctly, when we moved here, *you* were the one who wanted to have people around..."

That night, I went up to my room and found Matthias sitting at the desk. He seemed to be holding an invisible pen and writing in an invisible book.

"What are you doing?" I asked.

"Writing in my logbook. I'm recording the chores that I completed, and everything that happened here today. All those *visitors!*"

"You know, they have your logbook at the town museum. It's open so that people can read it."

He frowned. "Who on earth would want to read it?"

I shrugged. "I don't know. People who like lighthouses, I guess. And...people who are curious about what you did every day."

He looked puzzled. "Why are they curious about my profession? I am just an ordinary workman."

I shrugged again as Matthias snorted and turned back to his logbook. "These *tourists* nowadays don't seem to realize that we don't have *time* to just stand atop the lighthouse and admire the view. Our work is hard, and constant, and we cannot take any days off."

"Maybe they'll understand it if they read your book."

"Dylan, *I* don't understand why the visitors seem so fascinated by the lighthouse. They paint pictures of it! They photograph it! They read about it in their little tour guides. *Why?*"

"I don't know. Maybe...because it's pretty to look at? Or it's...historic? I mean, nobody builds lighthouses anymore."

"They *don't?*" He looked shocked. "That's a pity. Perhaps someday, lighthouses like this one will be all that's left of a *grand* and *glorious* era. And we light keepers may become obsolete."

I didn't tell him that that was exactly what happened. It might make him sad. So I just grinned and said that it would be funny if he would appear in some of the tourists' pictures.

"Do not even *joke* about such a thing, boy," he snapped, smacking his hand down on his invisible logbook. "Remember the ghost hunters and their cameras?"

I rolled my eyes and thought about that day. How could I forget it? Matthias had ranted about it for a week...

After Mom and Alondra had left for the pool one day, some ghost researchers came to visit, all loaded down with cameras and electronic stuff. They asked Dad if they could investigate all the stories they had heard about our haunted house, and the "sightings of a male apparition in early twentieth-century clothing." At least, that's what they said.

I wanted to warn Matthias, but couldn't find him anywhere. So, I watched as the ghost hunters wandered around and took pictures of the lighthouse and cottage, just like the tourists did. They didn't care about the buildings, though. They only wanted to see if "the spirit would manifest itself" and show up in their pictures. Before they left, they told Dad and me that they found some "low levels of spirit energy" around the chimney, but that was it. They sounded disappointed that they didn't see anything strange here.

I didn't see Matthias until that night, when he burst into our room, brushing soot off his hands. "I did *not* like what happened here today, Dylan! Not *one* little bit!" he shouted. "I had a *lot* of work to do today, until those…those…*ghost hunters* showed up…" He said "ghost hunters" as if they were dirty words. "I was forced to make myself scarce, so I hid in the chimney until they left. I *despise* those *ghost hunters* even more than *tourists!* They are just out seeking a thrill, at my expense. They chase me about my own property, and marvel at me as if I am an animal in a zoo. I am not a trained monkey, sent here for their amusement! Why can't they just let me be?"

"But I don't think they mean to bother you. Maybe they just want to talk to you, and learn about how you became a ghost."

"That's the problem! Dylan, I cannot even go about my daily routine without them attempting to study me. They call everything I do *paranormal activity.*"

"But at least the ghost hunters believe you exist. *Mom* still won't."

"Humph. *Ghost hunters.*"

Matthias turned around and disappeared, but I could still hear him grumbling about the ghost hunters as he drifted off to the lighthouse.

***

Another time, Matthias and I were just hanging out in my room, talking and listening to the radio. As Matthias complained about the music (he called it "a *hideous cacophony* that should be *outlawed*"), I opened the desk so I could look at the picture of the men on the boat. Matthias gasped and rushed over to me, pulling my hand away as he slammed the lid shut.

"Hey, hey, boy, what are you *doing* in there?" he cried. "You're messing up my paperwork!"

"What paperwork?" I asked, looking in the empty desk.

"*This* paperwork!" he barked. He pulled something out of the desk and waved it under my nose. Invisible papers rustled and fanned air into my face. "Property returns...expenditure logs...shipwreck reports...*oh*, and that is just the beginning. The only part of my job that I don't like is all the *paperwork*. Records, records, records."

"*Really?* I thought that you just cleaned the lighthouse, and turned it on every night."

Matthias chuckled. "There's a lot more to it than that, m'boy. Now, what were you looking for in my desk?"

It's not your desk anymore, I thought. But I just asked him if I could look at the picture.

"Do you mean this one?"

I stared as the picture appeared in his hand. "Y...*yeah*. How did you *do* that?"

He shrugged. "Why are you so fascinated by this photo-graph, sonny?"

"It's just a cool picture. I wish I knew who those people were."

"Dylan, that's *me!* Me and my dad. And I remember when this was taken. It was back in 1888, just before I started work-ing here. I was all of twenty years old. That was the year that they converted the lamp from using lard oil as fuel, to using kerosene. That was a big deal for us, then. It was *progress!*"

He sounded cheerful, but had a strange look on his face as he looked at the picture. "My mother was so proud when I was appointed Keeper here. She told me that I looked authoritative in my new uniform. The dear lady was relieved that she no longer had to worry about me going to sea with my father."

Matthias rubbed his eyes and handed me the picture. "I kept this in the desk so that every time I saw it, I would remember why I came here to work at the lighthouse. However, I have no use for it anymore. You may keep it."

"So, why did you come here to work -" I stopped and stared at the empty room. Matthias had disappeared. I knew that he was probably out doing his lighthouse stuff, and wanted to be left alone. I wondered why that picture seemed to upset him so much.

***

Although Matthias and I bothered each other sometimes, I didn't mind him living in my room anymore. He was an interesting roommate. He told me a lot of sea stories, and he taught me sea songs that I knew would really annoy Alondra. He taught me all about lighthouses and how to take care of them, and told me what it was like living here back in his time. He showed me how to tie all kinds of sailor's knots that Dad never even heard of. He even told me about his flock of chickens, his vegetable garden, and his cat, Missy, who kept the rats out of the chicken coop.

"...And those chickens and vegetables kept me from going hungry when the supply wagon couldn't make it out here to the Point with my provisions," he said. "We had some dreadful winters back in my day..."

One night, I told him about the boys who picked on me because I was short. "...They take my books and stuff away, and throw them on the floor. Then they push me around and tell me to go back to kindergarten. They say that I act like a girl because I like to read, and think I'm a geek because I like sailboats. They say that they're for sissies. None of them want to be my friend."

Matthias smiled, but it didn't look like he was laughing at me. He looked like he knew what I was going through.

"I think I can understand," he said softly.

"How? *You* don't have that problem. How tall *are* you, anyway?"

"I may not have the same problem as you do, but I know how it feels to have nobody like you. People don't like *me* now, because of what I am."

I was confused. "A...lighthouse keeper?"

"*No!* A *ghost!*"

I shrugged. Lately, I had been forgetting that he even *was* a ghost. Matthias was just...Matthias. He was the first real friend that I had ever had. I wasn't afraid of him anymore.

"Well, *I* like you."

"I'm glad to hear that. You're the only one who does." He looked at the floor and shook his head. "Let me tell you something, Dylan. I never expected to find myself stuck on the earth after I died. But after a while, I learned to take great pleasure in my ghostly abilities. For instance, I can do this." He vanished into a glowing little ball of light, which swooped through my room and bounced around like a tennis ball. I gasped. Was it the same light that had chased the men away from the lighthouse? Even though I knew that it was only Matthias, it still looked really spooky.

Soon, the light faded and he turned human again, looking proud of himself. "*That* is an *excellent* way to scare off trespassers."

"Well, it scared *me!* That was...like nothing I've ever seen before."

"Then I don't imagine that you've ever seen *this*, either." He stood up and snapped his fingers. The light flickered and went out, then popped back on again a second later. "And this..." He disappeared, and then reappeared on the other side of the room. "And due to my power of invisibility, over the years I have eavesdropped on many informative, and *scandalous* conversations."

"Well that's good, for you," I said. "But there's nothing good about being a little shrimp. All that's good for is that...I can fit into small spaces." I shrugged. "The things that *you* can do are cool. I hope when *I* die, I come back as a ghost."

"Believe me, sonny, you would *not* want to come back as a ghost." Matthias turned away and looked out the window. "It's a lonely existence. Imagine, going one hundred years with nobody to talk to. You are the only person with whom I have conversed since my death. It's rare that we find a mortal who's sensitive enough to interact with us, like yourself." He shrugged. "Perhaps that is why so many don't believe that we exist."

"Matthias? Is Uncle Zack...you know, um...still here? Like...like you?"

He shook his head. "Your uncle is no longer of this realm. He had nothing holding him here, whereas *I* have business to attend to. And I'll stay here and finish that if it takes another hundred years!"

***

The next morning, Mom and Alondra headed out to the car with their towels and gym bags. Mom smiled at me.

"Dylan, we're going to the pool. Would you like to come with us?"

"No. I'd rather stay here with Dad and Matthias."

Mom glanced at Dad and shook her head, and she and Alondra left for the pool.

Dad cleared his throat. "Um, Dylan, can you come with me for a minute? I'd like to talk to you."

I followed Dad as he walked past the lighthouse and out to the cliff, where he sat down. "Dylan, your mom's been kind of upset by some of the things that you've been talking about, lately. Would you like to tell me what's going on? What's up with this ghost that I hear so much about?"

"I told you before, Dad, I met the ghost who lives here. Matthias. But Mom won't believe me. She says there's no such thing, and I'm too old to have an imaginary friend. But he's *not* imaginary, Dad! He was a lighthouse keeper here. He was the last one who lived here, because when he became a ghost, he scared all the living ones away. But he liked Uncle Zack, so he never bothered him."

"*I* believe you, Dylan."

"Huh?"

"I said, *I believe you.* Everyone in town has always thought that there was something strange out here on the point. And *I* believe that there are more things in this world than we humans can ever know."

"*Really?*"

"Really." Dad looked out at the ocean, where a big schooner was sailing by. It looked like the same one that Matthias and I saw from the lighthouse top. People stood on the deck waving to us and taking pictures of the lighthouse. We waved back.

Dad looked at me and smiled. "So what is Matthias like?"

I thought for a moment. "Well, he's sort of grumpy, but nice. He always calls me *sonny*, or *boy*. I guess he's your age, because he has wrinkles around his eyes, and some gray hairs above his ears. He doesn't like ghost hunters, because they bother him, and he can't understand why the tourists like to take pictures of the lighthouse. But he likes to read – he's the one that took your detective book – and he can play the piano. He was the one playing it the other night. And he took Mom's dish towel to wash the windows in the lighthouse, and he was playing with the eggbeater because he said that he never saw an electric one before. He took your paint to paint the picket fence in the front yard – it's not there anymore, but *he* can still see it. And he put all of those ugly pictures back on the wall in Alondra's room, because he said he liked them there."

"Dylan, let me tell you what I think. It sounds to me like your friendship with Matthias is a very special thing. It's something that most people have never experienced, so they'll tell you that he's not real."

"Like Mom?"

"Yes. So please stop talking about him in front of your mom, OK? It's making her nervous. And she's worried about you."

"But she has nothing to worry about."

"I know. But Dylan...I hope that you won't be too disappointed when it's time for Matthias to move on. These kinds of things don't last forever."

"Aw, he would never leave the lighthouse. He'll always stay here to protect it."

Dad smiled and looked out at the ocean. But it was sort of a thoughtful smile, like he knew something that I didn't. "I'm sure he will, son. A part of him will always be here."

I didn't know what he meant, but was afraid to ask. So I jumped up and ran toward the house, calling to Dad over my shoulder. "I even have a picture of him! Wait."

I pounded up the stairs and pawed through the desk until I found the picture of Matthias on the boat. "See, here he is," I told Dad after I went back outside. "This was before he started working at the lighthouse. I tried to put it on my mirror, but Matthias doesn't like it there, because it makes him sad. He won't tell me why. I have to keep it in the desk."

Dad studied the picture, barely holding it by its edge. "Dylan, you need to be careful with this. It's from 1888; I'm surprised that it hasn't fallen apart. We should put it in a frame to keep it safe."

"Okay. Dad? Where do you think this was taken? And I wonder why he's standing on that boat with those nets. Think he was a sailor, or something?"

"That's an old fishing schooner, and it looks like it's in the harbor here. It's hard to say…but I know someone who I bet could tell you all about it."

"Who?"

"Come on," Dad said, digging in his pocket for his keys. "Let's take a walk."

Dad locked up the house, and we headed down the road, stopping at the town museum.

We were going to see Mrs. Cooper! I should've known.

Inside, we found her talking to a lady about some old quilts that were hanging up in another room. While we waited for her, I showed Dad the grumpy picture of Matthias.

"See, that's what he looks like now. Except, he's not mad, like he looks in that picture. And he doesn't have his hat on."

Dad didn't say anything and just kept looking from the snapshot to the portrait, like he was trying to memorize Matthias's face. Mrs. Cooper finished talking to the lady and hurried into the lighthouse room.

"Dylan and Roger! It's so nice to see you again. How are things out on the point? Have there been any...happenings?"

"Things couldn't be better, Mrs. Cooper," Dad said. "But Dylan found this old picture that he's been wondering about, and I knew that you were the best person to ask."

Even though I knew who was in the picture, I handed it to Mrs. Cooper and tried to act innocent. "Do you know anything about this guy?"

She put on a pair of glasses and peered at the picture. "Well! I've never seen *this* picture before! I'm going to guess that that's Mr. MacMurray as a young man. I can see it in his face." She turned it over and read the initials and date. "Yes, now I'm *positive* that's who it is. He was certainly a handsome young man. And the gentleman with the mustache might've been his father."

Dad glanced at me. "And Mr. MacMurray was the...lighthouse keeper, right?"

"Yes. His story was well known in our town's history. And it's a sad story that ended in tragedy."

"What kind of tragedy?"

"Well, Dylan, why don't you come over here to the desk and have a seat. You too, Roger." We pulled two chairs up to her desk as she began to talk.

"Everyone in town – even the children - called him by his first name, Matthias. He preferred it that way, so that's how I will refer to him, as well.

"Matthias was born in 1868, a few years after the end of the Civil War. He grew up here in Salvation Point. His father was a fisherman, and when Matthias was just your age, he went out on the boat to learn the trade. His father expected him to take over someday, but when Matthias was twenty, they were caught in a storm at sea. He was an excellent seaman by that time, and he was steering the boat. However, there was a terrible accident, and they collided with the cliffs below the lighthouse. His father was killed in the accident. Matthias tried to save him, but instead, he saw him die.

"Matthias was the only survivor of that wreck. He clung to the cliffs until the elderly lighthouse keeper rescued him the next morning. After that, he never went back to the sea. When the lighthouse keeper retired, Matthias decided to take his place. He wanted to have a chance to help people in danger on the water, and to save lives. For the rest of his life, he tried to make up for what he thought he did."

"But he didn't *do* anything wrong. It was an *accident*."

Mrs. Cooper shook her head. "That made no difference to him. He blamed himself because he couldn't save his father."

She stared down at the picture, which she held in both hands. "One night, many years later, there was a bad storm – a blizzard. Of course, Matthias had that lamp lit long before nightfall, but sometime during the night, he went out on the balcony outside the lantern room. The next day, his body was found down on the rocks with a broken neck. It was suspected that he had been blown over the railing just like a dry leaf.

"He was a good man, but a lonely and somber one. He never married, or had children. His death was such a tragedy. He died far too young."

Mrs. Cooper gave me back the picture and stared at me. "Why are you so interested in Matthias?"

I shrugged. "I dunno. I just liked the picture, I guess..."

She folded her arms. "Young man, I've worked with children all my life, and I know when I'm not being told the whole story."

"Should I tell her, Dad?"

"That's up to you. I'm not going to stop you."

I took a deep breath and looked down at the floor, sure that she would laugh at me when she heard the truth. "It's be-cause...I know him. He's my friend. And he's...he's the ghost of Salvation Point."

CHAPTER 8

Treasure Hunters

When I was outside the next morning, Uncle Zack's old lawn mower roared behind me as Dad pushed it back and forth across the grass. I had asked Dad if I could mow, but he said that I wasn't big enough yet. Then he waved me away and told me to go look for something to do, so I wandered out to the backyard with the metal detector.

As I headed toward the cliff, I thought about our trip back to the museum yesterday to see Mrs. Cooper. I had thought for sure that she'd tell me Matthias wasn't real, the way Mom did. Instead, she hugged me, and told me that she was proud of me for telling her the truth about Matthias. And *she* believed in him, too!

I hardly noticed when Matthias appeared, walking beside me and watching me with a puzzled look.

"What have you got there, sonny?" he asked.

"It's a metal detector. Haven't you seen it before? My dad bought it so we can look for the pirate treasure." I stopped and looked up at him. "Matthias? Did you ever hear about Captain Cutlass's treasure? It's supposed to be buried around here somewhere."

He snorted. "That's just an old legend! People have been telling the gullible tourists about that for years, trying to get them to come here. And Captain *Cutlass?* Now, what kind of a stupid name is that for a pirate?"

"Well, the Maine book that Dad gave me said that a cutlass was his favorite weapon, and he killed a lot of people with one. So that's how he got his name. His real name was…Thomas, I think."

Matthias frowned. "He sounds like a most unsavory fellow."

"Maybe. But if I find his treasure, I'll be rich! Do you want to help me look? I'll show you how to use this." I held the metal detector out to him, but he waved me away just like Dad did.

"I have a lot of work to do. I'm expecting a surprise visit from the inspector any day now. It's been a long time since he's shown up."

"Who's the *inspector?*"

Matthias shrugged. "Just one of my superiors. I need to keep this place looking shipshape, if I want him to give me a good report." He crouched down and pointed to a round, red pin on his collar. "Do you see this badge, sonny? It's called an Efficiency Star. I earned it from the inspector by keeping a *clean* lighthouse. I did not earn it by slacking off."

He straightened up and nodded toward the cliffs. "I have to get to work now, sonny. You remember to watch the tide. It will be coming in soon."

Matthias faded away, and a second later I saw him reappear at the top of the lighthouse.

I sighed and went back to treasure hunting, annoyed that Dad and Matthias didn't want me around. But soon I forgot about them when I found an Indian-head penny from *1902!* A few minutes later, I found a cool old button with a lighthouse on it.

I was squatting beside a tide pool and washing the mud off the button and penny, when I spotted two men climbing over the rocks.

One was as tall and skinny as Matthias, with greasy-looking hair slicked back into a ponytail. The other was shorter, chubby and bald, with a scruffy little beard on his chin and a long coat that flapped around in the breeze.

I gasped. He was the guy who'd been watching us the day we moved here!

He pointed at me and said something to the other guy, and they both headed toward me.

"*Hey*, what have we here?" he called. "A fellow *treasure* hunter?"

I glared at him and started climbing the path back up the cliff. "I don't talk to strangers."

That wasn't exactly true. After all, I had talked to Matthias when he was still a stranger, but that seemed different somehow. I didn't trust *these* men at all. They scared me.

The men looked at each other and stepped onto the path, blocking my escape. The rocks beside the path were too slippery to climb. And now the tide was coming in, just as Matthias said. I was trapped!

I could hear Dad's lawnmower circling the yard above the cliffs. Matthias was busy in the lighthouse. Mom was working on a painting on the other side of the yard, and I didn't care where Alondra was. I was all alone, and I guess the men knew it.

I gulped and looked up at them. They seemed to be ten feet tall as they puffed on their cigarettes and closed in on me, so near that I could smell their sweat.

"I'm Sleeter. Mel Sleeter," the bald guy said, jabbing his thumb against his chest. "And this here's my cousin, Quint."

"So now we're not strangers anymore," the skinny guy, Quint, said as he grinned at me. His teeth were all crooked and yellow. He needed to shave, too.

The man named Sleeter rocked back on his heels and squinted down at me over his fat belly.

"We are direct descendents of Captain Cutlass, one of the most *notorious* pirates in history."

"He was our great-grandfather, *many* times over."

"And *this* is a copy of his treasure map," Sleeter said, holding out a rolled-up paper. "The original one is over 200 years old; it was handed down through our family for generations. Betcha never seen anything like it, eh, pipsqueak?"

"I, uh…have to go home…"

They both chuckled as Sleeter unrolled the map and stuck it under my nose. "Look at this, little buddy. According to the map, Cutlass's treasure is buried somewhere on the Point, here! Millions of dollars in gold and jewels! And as direct descendents of our *illustrious* ancestor, his treasure *rightfully* belongs to *us*." Sleeter grinned at me, as the sun glistened on his shiny shaved head and gold earrings. He looked just like a pirate, himself.

Sleeter rolled up the map and stuck it back under his arm. "But we gotta be careful, digging treasure here. This place is haunted, you know. It's been said that there's a *really* nasty ghost here. Everybody knows that."

Quint snickered. "Yeah, the story goes that some dude fell off the tower and landed *right* about where you're standing.

Ker-splat!" He lunged at me and clapped his hands in my face, making me jump. They both laughed.

"And you know the only reason that *that* could've happened: he must've been drunk."

"He wasn't *drunk!*" I cried.

"He *wasn't*, eh?" Quint laughed and punched Sleeter's arm. "Ain't he sweet, Mel? He's so innocent." He sneered at me and tossed his cigarette butt in the water. "You'll understand those kind of things when you're older, kid."

I hated it when adults said that. How do *they* know how much I understand? And *these* two didn't even act like adults. They were just like the bullies in my class.

Sleeter looked up at the lighthouse and scratched his hairy chin. "I have big plans for that place. First, I'm tearing down the cottage, then the lighthouse, and then I can sell this property for *millions!* After I find the treasure, of course."

"You can't tear it down! I *live* there! My dad got it from my Uncle Zack."

"Oh, he *did*, did he?"

"And if the *lighthouse* isn't here, ships would crash into the rocks!"

Sleeter shrugged. "Who cares? That's their problem."

Matthias would care, I thought, but didn't say anything as Sleeter leaned over me and nodded at my hand. I had forgotten about the button and penny!

"Let's see whatcha got there, squirt."

I peeked into my hand to make sure they were both still there. "It's just an old button and – *HEY!*" I jumped away as Sleeter grabbed them out of my hand. "Those are *mine*, give 'em *back!*"

He gazed down at them with a greedy grin. "These'll get me a few bucks at the antique shop. Whaddaya say, Quint?"

"GIVE 'EM *BACK!*" I cried. I tried to grab them out of his hand, but he just snickered and held them above his head, where I couldn't reach.

Quint smirked at me. "You wouldn't tell your old *man* on us, now, would you, little guy?"

"Don't call me *little guy.*"

He snorted and elbowed Sleeter in the ribs. "Cute kid, huh?"

"And give me back my stuff. *I* found it."

Sleeter grinned again and stuck the button and penny in his coat pocket. "And what if I *don't?* You'll send the *ghost* after me?"

"Yeah, ya gotta watch out for the *ghost! Wooooooo!*" Quint howled.

"*You're* not afraid of a little old *ghost*, are you?" Sleeter asked.

"No. Are you?"

Sleeter laughed. "I'm not afraid of some old, dead lighthouse keeper!"

I caught a flash of something blue as Matthias's arm – just his arm – appeared, and grabbed Sleeter's map.

"WHOA, WHOA, QUINT, DID YOU SEE...WHAT IN THE-"

Sleeter stumbled away from me and watched as the map flew out to sea. It soared along on a gust of wind and landed in the waves far from shore.

"The map!" Sleeter cried, wading into the bay. "Quint, you idiot, help me get the *map!*"

But Quint couldn't help him. The rest of Matthias had appeared, and he grabbed Quint's ponytail and dragged him backwards towards a tidepool.

"NO! NOOOOO!" Quint screeched, clawing at the air and digging his sneakers into the rocks, his feet slipping and sliding as he struggled to escape. "Mel, get back here and *help me!*"

SPLASH! Quint tumbled into the tidepool and landed hard on the rocky bottom. Matthias towered over him as he sat up, sputtering and choking out the water he'd swallowed.

"You want to call me *drunk*, do you?" Matthias bellowed. "You *dare* to tarnish my reputation and threaten my job?"

Matthias folded his arms and watched as Quint staggered to his feet, dripping wet and covered with seaweed. Quint panicked and clutched his pulled hair, looking around for his invisible attacker.

I snickered. "You forgot to watch out for the *ghost*, Quint!" I called.

Matthias scowled at me and pointed up the path. "Don't just stand there, boy! Get on home!"

I grabbed my metal detector and scrambled up the path, looking back once more. Sleeter was swimming out to sea, trying to rescue his precious treasure map, while Quint scurried over the rocks, heading toward the road to town.

Matthias caught up to me as I headed to the house. "Dylan, wait!" he called.

I stopped as Matthias squatted down in front of me and looked me in the eye. "Are you okay?"

I nodded. "I am now. But they took the things that I found!"

"Do you mean these?" He held out his hand. In it sat the old button and penny.

"Yeah!" I cried, as Matthias dumped them into my hand. I thought I would never see them again. *"Thanks, Matthias!"*

I slipped the penny into my pocket and examined the button. The little lighthouse on it glittered in the sunlight as I compared it with the buttons on Matthias's coat. The button was dented and worn, but a perfect match. "Well, well. Looks like one of my successors lost a button," Matthias said.

"Do you think it's worth money?"

"Why would it be worth money? It's just a button."

"Because it's old. People like old stuff."

He shrugged. "Whether it's valuable or not, it seemed to be important to you. I couldn't allow those bullies to steal from a child."

"Yeah. Those guys are jerks."

"And they're *dangerous.* Don't forget that, Dylan. I've seen them poking around here at the lighthouse many times. They're nobody that you want to mess around with."

Were they the ones spying on us that night? I wondered. But I didn't say anything about that as we walked back to the house.

"Matthias? How could Quint threaten your job?"

He looked at me with a serious expression. "You see, Dylan, my employer, the U.S. Lighthouse Service, does not tolerate drunkenness. If a keeper is found intoxicated, he or she is fired immediately. I fear that if my superiors heard even a *rumor* of such misconduct, it could be all over for me."

I wondered if he would ever realize that he didn't have to worry about his "superiors" or the "inspector" anymore. They were all dead.

Matthias patted my shoulder. "I have to finish my chores now, Dylan. You must tell your parents what just happened. They won't let Quint and Sleeter get away with this."

He disappeared before I could argue with him. I guess he knew that I wasn't going to tell Mom and Dad *anything.* If I did, I knew that they wouldn't let me go outside by myself anymore.

I went up to my room and left the metal detector in the corner. I didn't feel like treasure hunting, now.

***

After dinner, I looked out the living room window as a beat-up black car chugged into the driveway. It was the longest car that I had ever seen, other than limos. I expected a tourist family to pile out of it and head for the lighthouse, but just one man got out and slammed the door. Even from the back, I recognized his shaved head and long flapping coat. *Sleeter!*

"Dad, there's somebody here," I called.

"They probably just came to look at the lighthouse."

"No...Dad, I think you need to go out there."

I guess I must've sounded scared, because Dad took one look at my face and headed out the front door. I followed close behind, wondering what was going on.

"Hey, what can I do for you?" Dad said with a smile, walking up to Sleeter. He stuck out his hand for him to shake.

Sleeter turned around. "Flint! Is that you?"

Dad gasped. *"Sleeter?"* Dad's hand dropped back to his side as they stared at each other, neither of them looking very friendly.

Matthias appeared beside me and we looked at each other, and then back at Dad and Sleeter. How did they already know each other?

Sleeter was quiet for a moment as he looked Dad up and down, like he was a bug. "So, I heard that you are the owner of this property?"

"Sure am," Dad said. "And who wants to know?"

Sleeter snorted. "Ain't that obvious, Flint? I came here with a proposal that I'm sure will make you very happy, since you -"

"Who's this?" Mom asked as she and Alondra came outside. Mom smiled at Sleeter and introduced herself. "Well, Mr. Sleeter, won't you come in?"

"Er...no. As I was saying to your husband, I am sure that you will be very pleased with what I have to offer you today."

"Yeah? And what is that?" Dad sounded suspicious as Mom gave him a dirty look. It was the same look that she always gave me that meant, *don't be rude.*

"*That,* Flint, is a little real estate deal that will...ahem... make you even *richer* than you *evidently* already are. "

"Whatever you're proposing, Sleeter, I'm not interested. Now -"

"Look, Flint, you haven't even heard my offer! I am willing to pay two-hundred and fifty-thousand dollars for the cottage, lighthouse, and land -"

Dad held up his hand. "I don't want to hear it. I can see you've never changed, even after all these years, Sleeter."

"*Roger!*" Mom gasped.

"Rorianne, this place has been in my family since I was a kid, and someday I'm going to leave it to Dylan and Alondra. It's not for sale at any price!"

"Oh, you *are* a greedy one, aren't you, Flint? Okay. I am pre-pared to offer you half-a-million dollars for this place. That's my final offer."

Dad looked at Sleeter's junky old car. "*No,* and I mean, no. But even if I were interested, I can see that *you* don't have that kind of money."

"Oh-*ho,* really?" Sleeter took a step back and stared at Dad, as if he couldn't believe what he said. "Just because I'm not a hotshot from the big city, like you, doesn't mean that I don't have the money!"

Alondra gazed at Sleeter with a big smile. "Oh, take the money, Daddy, *please,* take it," she babbled. I rolled my eyes, but Dad ignored her.

Sleeter scowled. "*Look* at you, with your brand-new *vehi-cle,* and your big fancy sailboat. I'm so *sick* and *tired* of you out-of-state people from the city, buying up all of our land and trying to tell us how to run our town!"

"Sleeter, I'm not from the city, you know that. We're back for the summer -"

"Just for the *summer?* Big deal. I remember you, Flint. You got married and moved out of here to *make it big* in New York *City.* You're not one of us anymore. You're nothing more than a *tourist* now. Just a *summer* person. Why don't you take your wife and brats and go back where you belong?"

Dad narrowed his eyes and glared at the man. "Sleeter, it's time for you to leave. You're not going to talk that way in front of my family."

Sleeter stepped up to Dad and poked his finger in his chest. "This is not over, Flint," he growled.

I looked up at Matthias as he loosened his tie and pushed up his sleeves. "Stand back, sonny. This might not be pretty."

I stared as Matthias rushed at Sleeter and starting shaking him by his coat collar. "Did you not hear the man?" Matthias yelled. "He already told you that he is not interested in your proposal! This summer, he and his family have taken good care of this place that provides my home and employment, and I approve of their presence here. I bid you good day, and do not bother them again with your folly!"

Matthias's shouts filled the yard as Sleeter's head jerked back and forth, his eyes wild. Sleeter screamed and started swinging his fists in Matthias's direction, even though I knew that he couldn't see him. But his fists just passed through Matthias's body without hurting him. After that, Sleeter stopped punching and stared straight ahead, his mouth hanging open.

Matthias twisted Sleeter's arm up behind his back and pushed him to his car. "Begone with you!" he shouted, shaking his fist in Sleeter's face as he shoved him into the driver's seat.

Dirt sprayed out from under the tires as Sleeter tore down the road and sped off to town.

Mom stared after the car, stunned.

"*Roger*, what just happened here? Who *was* that? And why was that man punching at thin air?"

"That's *Mel Sleeter*," Dad muttered. "I've known him since I was a kid; he was in my class all through school. He was the biggest bully around, and he tormented me for years. Looks like he hasn't changed at all."

"No, no, I didn't mean *him!* Didn't you hear that *voice?* It was the voice of a stranger, a man -

"You *heard* him, Mom? That was *Matthias!*"

"Not *now*, Dylan!" Mom snapped.

"Um...Rorianne, maybe you should listen to our son," Dad said. "We are the only ones...*visible* here. If that voice didn't belong to Sleeter, or any of us, then who was it? It could *only* have been Matthias -"

"Oh, *Roger!*" Mom threw her hands in the air. "You are the most *exasperating* man! Sometimes you make me so *mad!*"

She turned and stomped toward the house, Alondra trailing behind her.

Dad just shook his head and watched them leave. I tapped his arm.

"Uh, Dad? I was afraid to tell you this, but...um, that guy was already here this morning. He and his friend – his cousin, I mean – were talking to me, down on the rocks."

Dad looked startled. He knelt down and put his hands on my shoulders. "They were talking to you? Son, tell me what they said!"

I shrugged. "They told me that they were looking for Captain Cutlass's treasure. I guess he's like their great-grandpa, or something. But then they started making fun of Matthias.

They said that he was drunk when he fell off the lighthouse. Then they laughed about it. And Sleeter said that he didn't care if a ship crashes into the rocks."

Dad frowned. "That sounds just like something that Sleeter would say."

"And I had found these in the yard..." I dug into my pocket and pulled out the button and penny. "Sleeter stole them right out of my hand."

Dad gasped. "He *stole* them from you?"

"Yeah. He was going to sell them to the antique shop, but Matthias got them back for me."

Dad looked at the button and penny. I could tell that he was getting even angrier at Sleeter, but he took a deep breath and spoke in a calm voice. "Then it sounds like Matthias is a good friend to you."

"He *is*, I guess. Even though he doesn't believe the story of Captain Cutlass. But *Sleeter's* a creep. I'm not sure that I want to live here now, if people like Sleeter are here."

"People like Sleeter are everywhere. You shouldn't judge the whole town by the actions of one person. We can't let him scare us away, and ruin our summer here."

"But he thinks that the treasure is buried under the light-house. And he wants to tear our house down!"

"Listen to me, Dylan. *Nobody* is going to tear the house down. And we're not leaving here until it's time to go home." Dad straightened up and looked at me. "Now, go on back inside. I need to have a talk with your mom."

CHAPTER 9

Rat Island

A few days later, I went downstairs and found Dad loading our fishing poles, the cooler, and the gas stove into the car. "Where are you going?" I asked.

"Sailing," Dad said with a grin. "I thought that you and I could go out to Rat Island today. Remember, I promised that I'd take you there sometime."

"*Yes!*" I cried, punching the air. "Are Mom and Alondra coming, too?"

"Nope, it'll be just the two of us. Your mom wanted to finish that big painting that she's been working on, and Alondra..." Dad rolled his eyes. "Let's just say that she wants no part of it. Now, go get dressed, and eat some breakfast while I finish loading the car."

I scampered back upstairs and changed into my clothes, grabbed the old binoculars and compass, and was ready five minutes later.

"Mom, guess what?" I said, when I found her washing some paint brushes in the kitchen sink. "We're going to Rat Island!"

Mom made a face. "I know; your father told me. And that's such an *atrocious* name for an island. It doesn't sound very appealing."

"Well, Dad told me that the man who named it thought it was shaped like a big rat, all hunched over. That's why it's called Rat Island."

"That man must've had quite an imagination, but *I'm* not going anywhere that's named after *rats*."

Good, I thought. But I didn't say anything as I choked down my soggy cereal and waited for Dad to get ready.

As I was getting into the car a few minutes later, I had a *great* idea! "Dad, hold on! I'm gonna invite Matthias to come with us!"

"Dylan, I don't think Matthias can..." I couldn't hear the rest of whatever Dad said as I raced up to my room.

I found Matthias standing next to the stuffed seagull, arranging its ruffled feathers back into place. "Matthias, guess what? Dad's bringing me out to the *island!* Just me and him – Mom and Alondra won't be there to spoil things. We're gonna go fishing, and have a cookout, and maybe look for the treasure! Wanna come?"

He frowned. "I am not allowed to leave the light station without permission from my superiors."

"You're kidding. *Really?*

"Either myself, or an assistant must remain on the premises at all times."

"You can't even go into *town*, or *anything?*"

Matthias shrugged. "Not without permission."

I just stared at him. "But you're a *man*, not a little kid. How can they tell you that?"

"Dylan, are you ready to go?" Dad called.

"Hey, if you change your mind, we'll be at Rat Island. Dad said it's to the north-west -"

"I know that island well," Matthias said as he turned back to the seagull. "Go have fun."

At the harbor, I helped Dad load our stuff into *Rorianne Rose's* cabin. Then I looked down at *Thunder*, tied to the dock, rocking and swaying in the waves that barely moved Dad's big boat.

"Can I follow you with *Thunder?*"

Dad shook his head. "Not today, Dylan. The island is three miles out to sea. It can get too rough out there for a little boat like *Thunder*. But I'll tell you what. I'll let you steer, this time." I grinned and climbed aboard.

Dad frowned. "Aren't you forgetting something?" he asked as he held my life vest out to me.

"Aw, Dad, do I *have* to wear it? It's *hot* out."

He shrugged. "That's your choice; you know the rule. No jacket, no boat."

I sighed, but clipped the life jacket around me as Dad untied *Rorianne Rose* and swung himself aboard. We left the harbor and headed into the open ocean, joining the other boats that cruised along under the hot sun. Dad and I played a game that we made up, where he pointed out different sailboats we passed, and I had to identify them in under five seconds. "...That's a ketch," I said. "That one's a yawl...and there's that schooner that we see all the time! The windjammer."

"Very good," Dad said with a smile. "I haven't been able to stump you in quite a while, now."

We sailed along until a gust of wind slammed the sail from one side of the boat to the other. "DUCK!" Dad yelled as the boom zipped over my head and almost tipped us over.

"Don't let her jibe!" Dad said after he helped me get the boat back under control. "That boom could swing around and knock you overboard…or knock you out." He shrugged. "Or both!"

I scowled at the boom, determined not to let it happen again. The boom's the pole attached to the bottom of the mast, and it holds the bottom of the sail. It swings back and forth over the boat, so you can adjust the sail to catch the wind. Dad always warned me to stay out of its way. Now I understood why.

"Why don't you let me take the tiller, Dylan, we're almost to the island," Dad said. "See, it's right over there."

"Look, there's a cabin up there," I said, as I pointed to the side of the hill.

"Yes. A ranger lives there all summer, and takes care of the island. It's all woods. Except for the cabin and the hiking trails, and the new docks that were built a while back, the island's never changed." Dad seemed happy about that.

We pulled up to the empty dock and tied up *Rorianne Rose*. "Looks like we might have the place to ourselves," Dad said, as I helped him carry our stuff over to a picnic spot back in the trees. Dad said they were spruces and firs, like the ones near our house. It was nice and cool under the trees. They smelled good, too.

"Can I go look around?"

"If you be careful. There are miles of trails here, and it's easy to get lost. Stay on this main trail, where you can always see the water. Later on, we'll go for a hike up in the woods, okay?"

"Sure, Dad." I hung my binoculars around my neck and grabbed my compass.

"You should leave your binoculars and compass in the boat, Dylan. They're too valuable for you to be playing with."

"But I might need them."

Dad just sighed. "Well, don't go too far. Our burgers will be ready soon."

I started down the main trail, which followed the rocks along the water. Seagulls screeched and soared, and some seals lounged on a rocky island offshore. I put the binoculars to my eyes and finally spotted our lighthouse, standing white and clean against the dark trees of the nature preserve.

As I headed back down the trail, the brush started growing thicker along the shore. But I kept seeing a flash of blue and white – like a t-shirt and jeans, rustling through the bushes, not far behind. Was someone following me? I looked back at the empty trail and started to jog. I didn't dare to turn back.

"Hey, kid. C'mon over here," a man called.

I jumped and took off running. I knew that voice...

Sleeter!

He wasn't even trying to hide, now. He stepped into the middle of the trail, laughing, and I kept looking back until I rounded a bend and couldn't see him anymore.

But I knew that he was still behind me. *Why?* What did he want?

I didn't want to find out.

I finally stopped to catch my breath, sweat dripping off my face. I just wanted to get back to Dad!

A twig snapped behind me. I gasped and looked up, ready to run.

"I *know* you're here, little buddy. Come out, come out, wherever you are!" Sleeter sang. I knelt behind a rock and watched as he mumbled something and spit on the ground. He looked all around, then turned and walked away. I waited until he was out of sight, then bolted into the woods until I couldn't see the water anymore.

The dark woods seemed to swallow me up as I darted among the tree trunks, looking for a place to hide. It was *creepy* in those woods. And quiet...*too* quiet. I couldn't even hear the waves or the seagulls anymore. Instead, some little bird called in the trees as the prickly branches tossed in the wind and scraped against my arms. I tried to find my way back to the trail without meeting up with Sleeter, but the trees and rocks all looked the same to me.

Then I remembered: my compass! I reached into my jeans pocket and found...nothing. My fingers just poked through a big hole in the cloth. The compass was gone!

"Oh, *no*," I muttered as I tried the other pocket and came up with nothing. Dad had *told* me not to play with it! I guess he was right.

For a moment, I forgot about Sleeter and started wandering through the trees, searching the ground. I hoped that I was heading back the way I came...

A strong hand grabbed my shoulder. I yelped and spun around, but there was nobody there. Nobody I could see, anyway.

"Matthias?" I whispered.

He appeared beside me.

"Don't *do* that!" I cried. "Sleeter is here!"

He nodded. "I know. That's why I've come. He's been watching you, and waiting until he catches you alone."

What was he going to do if he caught me alone? I wondered.

"Matthias, I tried to get away and hide, but all these stupid trees look the same, and now I got a hole in my pocket, and I'm lost, and I can't find my *compass!*"

"Don't you mean...*my* compass?" I was surprised when he opened his hand and held out the shiny brass compass with the initials on top. "You need to be more *careful* with things, boy. I just found this on the ground. "

Matthias grabbed my wrist and slapped the compass into my hand, closing my fingers around it. "That belonged to my father, Michael. I inherited it upon his death." He shrugged. "I guess it's yours, now."

"*Really?* Thanks, Matthias." I held up the compass and brushed some dirty pine needles off the top. The brass was still clean, though, and it shone in the dim light under the trees.

"I wonder how Sleeter got out here? I didn't hear a boat coming."

"That's because he paddled out here in a sea kayak."

I snickered. "How did he fit into a *kayak?* He's so *fat.*"

"Dylan, that's rude."

"But he *is.* I feel sorry for the kayak."

"Enough of that! Let's go."

"But how did you know I got lost? And what about your superiors?"

He shrugged and stared off into the woods for a second. "This is the first time that I have left the light station in so... so *long,*" he whispered. "It is a most odd feeling, and I do realize that I might incur disciplinary action from my superiors. I could even lose my job. However, it is most important to keep you safe. Come, now. Sleeter is near."

I grabbed his sleeve. "Don't leave me alone!"

"Don't worry; I'm not going anywhere. Not until you get back to your father."

I took his hand and wouldn't let go as he led me down the trail. I knew that I was acting like a baby, but I was too scared of Sleeter to care. I didn't want Matthias to leave me alone in these creepy woods, either.

"You all have it easy, nowadays," he said after a few minutes. "When I was a boy, my family and I would come out here and have picnics. My dad, uncles, cousins…sometimes, even some of the ladies. But there were no trails here then, or tables or outhouses, or a dock to tie up our boat. It was just a wild island…"

When I heard a noise in the bushes nearby, I gasped and spun around without letting go of Matthias. I spotted Sleeter slinking through the trees alongside Matthias and me, as silent as a wolf. Like he was…stalking me.

"He's following us!" I whispered.

"Shh. Don't panic and just keep walking."

"Can he see you?"

Matthias nodded and didn't say another word as Sleeter stopped short and stared at us. We walked right below the ledge that he was standing on, but he didn't come after me.

I looked up at Matthias. He seemed to be concentrating hard on something. I knew that Sleeter was watching us as we continued down the trail, even though I didn't see him again. But Matthias didn't relax until we reached the clearing and I saw Dad at our picnic table.

"Dylan! Where've you been? The food is getting cold! Now, do you want a burger, or a hot dog?"

"Um…I, um…both, I guess." I shrugged and headed for the picnic table as Matthias walked beside me, nodding down at me with a little smile. I was safe, now. I finally let go of his hand.

"Dad!" I cried, turning away from Matthias and touching Dad's arm. "When I was out in the woods, I saw -"

"*Whoa*, Dylan, your hand is *ice cold!*" Dad yelped. "What'd you do, stick it in the cooler?"

I shrugged. Maybe it would be better not to tell him about Sleeter.

"Um…so what did you see?" Dad handed me my paper plate of food and red plastic cup of Coke.

"*Matthias!*" I said, trying to smile and pretend that nothing was wrong. "He came with us, after all! See, he's right -" I looked up at empty air beside my bench. Matthias was gone. "There." I sighed and bit into my burger.

I was disappointed that Matthias didn't stay for our picnic, but at least he *did* bring me back to Dad, like he said he would. And then I didn't let Dad out of my sight for the rest of the day. We went fishing, but didn't catch anything. Then we hiked all around the island, coming back on a trail through the woods. I wasn't scared to be in the woods then, since Dad was with me. He told me the names of some flowers and birds that we saw, but I didn't say much. Dad asked me if I was feeling okay, so I kept pretending that nothing was wrong, even though I knew that Sleeter might have been spying on us. And that took all the fun out of the rest of the day.

After our hike, we loaded up the boat to head home. Dad raised the mainsail, and…

"Dad, look!" I cried.

"What in the world!" he gasped.

Long tears were slashed into the cloth, from top to bottom, fluttering like ribbons in the breeze. The wind blew right through the holes and rips. The sail was useless, now.

"Dylan...look at this!" Dad whispered. "It's *ruined!*" He sank down on the seat near the cabin door and rubbed his face.

"It was Sleeter!" I cried. "It *had* to be him! He was here, Dad, here on the island, and he was following me through the woods! I got lost trying to get away from him, but Matthias brought me back. Sleeter must've did this when me and you were hiking!"

Dad shook his head. "Dylan, why didn't you tell me all this before?"

I just shrugged as Dad sighed and examined the jib, the smaller sail at the front of the boat. Even that had been slashed.

"Will we have to stay here overnight?" I asked. "We have our sleeping bags in the cabin, and we can catch fish to eat for breakfast, or...hey! Can't you call for help on the radio?"

"No, we're not staying overnight, son," Dad mumbled. He looked so sad as he stared at the ruined sails. "In all my life, I never would've thought that I'd have to worry about someone vandalizing my boat, way out here." He gulped. "I guess times have changed, Dylan. This town really isn't the same as I remembered."

He plodded down into the cabin and pulled up a hatch in the floor, lifted out a small outboard motor and carried it to the deck. It was so rare that Dad had to use it – and always just during times when the wind died down to nothing – that I forgot that he had the emergency motor.

"It was a good thing that your mother made me buy this when I first started taking you out sailing when you were little," he grunted as he fastened it to the back of the boat. "I think there's enough gas in here to get us home. Now, what was this about Sleeter following you through the woods?"

I tried to explain as little as I could so I wouldn't make Dad worry. If he knew what happened, he wouldn't let me go out by

123

myself anymore! And if *Mom* knew…*she'd* make us all pack up and move back to the city.

I was surprised when Matthias appeared on the seat beside me. He chuckled. "I placed Sleeter's kayak paddle up in a tree. He'll be stranded here, for a while. Perhaps he will learn his lesson."

Matthias disappeared before I could answer him.

Dad started the noisy little motor, and as we headed back, I spotted Sleeter jumping up and down on the shore, waving his arms and screaming at us. Dad didn't see him, but I grinned and waved at him as we drove away. He looked furious! I was glad that I couldn't hear what he was saying.

It was funny that Sleeter got stranded here, but I didn't tell Dad about it. He still looked really upset. I felt sorry for him. He had tried so hard to make this a fun day for me, but Sleeter ruined it all. I knew that our summer here in Salvation Point would never be the same, again.

CHAPTER 10

Kidnapped

A week after Dad and I went to the island, I headed down our road after lunch, repeating the list of things that I needed to buy at the store. "Milk, hamburger meat, a dozen eggs, macaroni..." I mumbled. I took a marker out of my pocket and wrote the list on my hand. Mom *hated* it when I did that, but it didn't matter, now. This was the first time that she was letting me walk to town by myself! She gave me some extra money to get an ice cream, too, after warning me to be *very* careful and come *straight* home. She looked nervous.

I wondered *why* Mom was so worried about letting me walk to town on my own. After all, when we were back home in the city, she had no problem with me going to the corner store alone. I guess Dad made a big mistake when he told her what happened on the island. I remembered how she and Dad talked about it that morning, after I asked if I could go.

"*...I promise you, honey, Dylan is safer here in Salvation Point than he is on the streets of New York City,*" Dad had told her. "*It's a small town; people watch out for each other, here. It's perfectly safe for him to walk to the store. He's growing up, Rorianne; you need to stop treating him like a baby...*"

"*But Sleeter!*" Mom cried. "*You said that he vandalized the boat so badly that you had to order new sails! And then, he followed Dylan through the woods! And what was that all about, anyway, Roger? You were supposed to be watching him! It was extremely irresponsible of you to allow Dylan to go off by himself! Especially now that we know that that...that sleazy Sleeter is hanging around...*"

"*Sleeter's a coward, Rorianne. He wouldn't dare to bother Dylan in town, with other people around...*"

They started arguing about it, but Dad finally talked Mom into letting me go. I don't know how he did it...but he did.

Out on the bay, a nice-looking red sloop tacked into the wind. The waves lapped on the rocks, and birds tweeted in the woods. I grinned. I was finally free! It would've been more fun if Matthias could come with me, but I didn't bother to ask him. I knew that he'd say his "superiors" wouldn't let him leave, so I just left him home.

It didn't take long to reach the general store. A little bell jingled above my head as I pushed open the glass door. The cool air conditioning dried the sweat off my arms as I started down the aisles, gathering up my things.

"OK, look. I'll tell you about the guy at the lighthouse. That kid's father. He refuses to sell..."

I jumped. I *knew* I'd heard that voice somewhere. I peeked down the next aisle and saw...Sleeter! *Sleeter and Quint!* I zipped back around into my aisle and listened in.

"His name's Flint – Roger Flint. He's a sailor, and he's got this sailboat, the *Rorianne Rose*, over in the harbor." Sleeter snickered. "But I took care of *that*, didn't I? What good is a sailboat without a sail?"

Quint shrugged. "So whaddaya want me to do with him?"

"You know what I want, Quint! I want that treasure! The map and GPS coordinates tell me that we'll find it right there, somewhere near the lighthouse. I'll tear that tower down by myself, if I have to!"

"I've already told you that you can't *do* that! The lighthouse is still used every night! The *government* runs it -"

"Listen, Quint." Sleeter lowered his voice, but I could still hear him. "Don't you mess this up for me! Look, do you want half the money, or not? The backhoes and excavators are all ready to go, so I can start to dig anytime. Now I just need the deed to that land! I want those people *out* of there, so I can start searching. I don't care what you do. Just get Flint where it'll hurt him the most!"

"And what's *that* supposed to mean?"

"Think about it. He's got those kids. And that little brat of his knows all about our plan. He's probably telling everyone."

Quint held up his hands and backed away. "Don't look at me. *I* ain't the one who told him."

"Well, how was *I* supposed to know that his old man owned the place? So now we need to shut him up. *Permanently!*" Sleeter chuckled and rubbed his hands together. "I would've nabbed him when I saw him on the island the other day, but there was some guy walking with him. And you should've seen him: he wasn't dressed for a walk in the woods. He was all dressed up like...I don't know, a sea captain, or something. He was wearing a *tie*, and some kind of a fancy jacket. He was prob'ly from the big city, just like them." Sleeter shrugged. "I guess we'll just have to wait 'till we catch the kid alone."

I gasped as I realized just what Sleeter meant. Was he planning to…kidnap me? *Kill* me? My arms wobbled as I lost my hold on the groceries, and everything clattered to the floor. The macaroni fell with a rattle and crash, the eggs shattered, one by one, splattering yolks and slime across the floor, and *SPLOOSH!* The carton of milk burst open and exploded all over my jeans. I knelt in the mess, trying to pick everything up before Sleeter and Quint noticed me…

"Well, look who we have here," Sleeter called. "It's the little guy himself!" I looked over at the two of them, who were leaning against the shelves at the other end of the aisle, smirking meanly at me.

"Cleanup on aisle three!" Quint sang, snickering.

A cold breeze blew down the aisle as Matthias appeared beside me. "Matthias, you're here!" I cried. "I'm sure glad to see you -"

"Shh!" He squatted down so we were face-to-face. "Dylan, listen to me. You need to get out of here, *now.*"

"But my stuff!"

"Never mind that, just follow me. Hurry!"

Matthias grabbed my hand and pulled me toward the front door. I had to run to keep up with him. He drifted through the door without letting go of my hand, and –

THUNK!

I crashed into the glass door and fell on the floor, holding my nose. Blood started running out from between my fingers. I looked up and saw Matthias on the other side of the door, staring down at me with his hands over his mouth. He looked as shocked as I felt.

One of the checkout ladies came rushing over to me. "Oh, honey, you're hurt!" she cried. "Someone get me some Kleenex; this little boy is bleeding -"

"I'll take care of him, lady," Sleeter said, following her to the front door. "He's my nephew. I'll get him home safe."

"I'M *NOT* HIS NEPHEW!" I wailed.

Matthias opened the door, grabbed my shirt, and pulled me to my feet. "I am so truly sorry that you're injured!" he said as we fled across the parking lot. "It was my fault. I often forget the limitations of a mortal body."

The checkout lady shrieked. "Did you *see* that? The door just opened by *itself!*"

I looked back and saw Sleeter charging at me. "Kid, you get back here!" he yelled. "I just want to talk to you a minute!"

"DYLAN, RUN!" Matthias gave me a shove towards the road home.

I looked back once more, to see Sleeter tripping over Matthias's feet and Quint getting thrown against a tree. Matthias slugged them both in their faces. "*That* was for harassing and robbing the boy, and insulting me last week!" he shouted.

Quint and Sleeter escaped from Matthias and ran for their car, panicking as they stumbled around and bumped into each other.

Then I turned and ran.

***

I didn't get far when I heard their car squealing out of the parking lot and speeding up the road. I looked left and right for a place to hide. There was an abandoned house just ahead, hidden behind some big bushes. I jumped over the ditch beside the road and landed in the tall grass.

I crouched down into the grass and crawled toward the house, trying to catch my breath and ignore the mosquitoes that buzzed around my head. Mom had been right: I shouldn't have gone to town by myself! I was all alone out here, and didn't know if I'd make it home now that Sleeter and Quint were after me...

Where was *Matthias?* Why didn't he stop them? And didn't the checkout lady and the other people at the store hear them chasing me?

My heart pounded and sweat trickled into my eyes as Sleeter's big black car crept closer to the house with its windows down. I thought that they spotted me, but the car continued down the road.

I didn't want to leave the abandoned house. They could come back any second! I looked up at an empty window above my head. If only Matthias was around to lift me up there! If I could just get into the house, I'd find a better place to hide...

I grabbed the windowsill and tried to climb in, but wasn't tall enough. For a minute, I hung there by my hands as I felt around for footholds on the worn-out siding. But when the rotting windowsill crumbled under my hands, I lost my hold and fell back down in the weeds.

"Lookin' for us?"

Someone snickered as I gasped and looked up – *way* up – at a man who loomed over me, looking down at me with his hands in his pockets. I just stared from his dirty old sneakers, up to his ripped jeans, sweaty undershirt, and stubbly face surrounded by long, greasy hair. *Quint!*

He grinned, showing his crooked yellow teeth. "Why don'tcha take a ride with us, little man? We ain't gonna hurt-cha. We got some *candy* for you in the car!"

"I don't want your candy!" I yelled, as I jumped to my feet and backed away. Did he think I was so dumb that I would fall for the old *candy* trick?

As Quint began to laugh, I spun around and ran...straight into Sleeter. He grabbed my arms and lifted me off my feet, even as I kicked at him and screamed for Matthias.

"You want to do this the hard way, eh, squirt?" Sleeter grunted. He tossed me over his shoulder the way Dad did, but he wasn't playing around. "LET ME GO!" I screamed, pounding his back with my fists.

Sleeter pulled some keys out of his pocket and tossed them to Quint. "You drive."

Quint looked surprised. "You're not *really* gonna *do* this, are you, Mel? I thought we was just tryin' to scare the kid."

"Just shut up and get in the car! And do what I say! *Both* of you!"

"MATTHIAS!" I screamed as Sleeter carried me to the car. "DAD! SOMEBODY, HELP ME –"

"Knock it off, you little punk!" Sleeter snarled, yanking open the back door. He leaned over and threw me behind the front seats.

"NO! LET ME *GO!*" I squirmed up on the back seat and reached for the door.

"Get back on the floor!" Sleeter bellowed. He grabbed my shirt and threw me onto my stomach, screaming at me not to move. I looked over my shoulder as he plopped down in the backseat above me. There was no escape, now.

Quint started the car and pulled away. I was glad that Sleeter couldn't see my face as I started to cry. I couldn't help it.

"Here, kid, hold this over your nose." I squirmed away as Sleeter bent down and shoved a greasy old rag into my face.

"I didn't know that you cared so much about the kid, Mel," Quint said.

Sleeter shrugged. "I don't. I just don't want his blood all over my car."

What blood? I wondered. I gasped as I looked down and saw that my bloody nose had dripped all over the front of my shirt!

I pushed the rag away and tried to calm down. I hoped Sleeter wouldn't notice as I looked around my little prison.

The car was trashed. A little *blood* wouldn't make it any messier than it already was. Some stale potato chips crunched underneath me, and cigarette butts lay crumpled in the corner. My nose filled with the greasy stink of an old fast-food wrapper that was wadded under the front seat. A rotting apple rolled up to my face and brushed its slimy skin against me as Quint turned a corner. I reached up and batted the apple away, then put my hand down on something sticky – a half-eaten lollipop, gummy from the hot summer.

Oh, yuck, I thought. Now my hand was covered with lollipop goo and the sand that covered the floor. I tried to wipe the mess off on my jeans.

"Hold still!" Sleeter snapped, stomping on my leg. I yelped and scrunched as small as I could behind the driver's seat.

I stayed quiet for a minute as I looked through a rusted-out hole in the floor, watching the road whiz by under my nose. "Where are you taking me?"

Sleeter laughed. "Far away, kid. Far, far away. If your old man ever wants to see you again, he'll give me what I want. Once he hands over the deed, he gets his kid back."

"But how do you know that the treasure is really buried there?"

"Shut up, kid."

Quint sounded worried as he spoke up from the front. "I'm telling you, Mel, you've gone too far this time. I don't want to be a part of this anymore."

"Too late now, Quint! Just drive!"

Sleeter lit up a cigarette and sprawled out in the seat. "*Nobody* makes a fool of *me*, kid!" he growled. "Especially no rich, big-city tourist like your old man! I *know* that he stole my kayak paddle last week, and he's going to pay! If it weren't for a lobsterman giving me a ride back from the island, I'd still be out there now.

"And I don't know how your old man did all those things when I was at your house that day...when he made that weird voice come out of nowhere, and when he twisted my arm behind my back, and made those hands start shaking me..."

"Hands?" Quint sounded puzzled.

"I wasn't talking to *you*, peabrain," Sleeter snapped. "I already *told* you about it the other night! It was like some kind of...of an *invisible force* was attacking me! But we *all know* that that's *impossible*, don't we? Even out there on that Point, where it's *supposedly* overrun with ghosts, and evil spirits..." Sleeter laughed. "Now look, kid, I *know* that it was your old man who must've done some kind of...I don't know, crazy *illusions*, or *magic tricks*, or whatever. What is he, some kind of a demented ventriloquist?"

"My dad's not demented," I whimpered.

Sleeter snickered. "Can you get a load of this kid, Quint? He thinks he's tough, mouthing off to me, but he won't be so tough if I *hurt* him! And I just might have to hurt him anyway, if his old man don't cough up the deed!"

"That's *not cool*, Mel," Quint said. "You don't have to hurt him."

"Shut up and drive, Quint. *I'll* do the talking here!" Sleeter shouted. "Ya hear that, kid? Your pal ain't here to protect you, now!"

"Yes I am," Matthias whispered.

I peeked over my shoulder and saw him sitting between Sleeter and me. I felt a little braver, now that Matthias was in the car.

The trip seemed to take forever. It was hot lying on the floor, smelling all the disgusting smells, and feeling the sand and cigarette butts stick to my sweaty arms. Quint went around all the corners too fast, and I thought I was going to throw up. I squeezed my eyes shut and held my breath...

"Step on it!" Sleeter bellowed. "What're you slowing down for?"

"There's chickens in the road, Mel."

"Then run 'em over!"

When the car stopped, Sleeter lunged over the front seat and started screaming at Quint. I looked up and slowly reached for the door handle...

"Don't try it, sonny," Matthias whispered, closing his hand over mine.

I was disappointed, but knew that he was right. I had to wait for a better time to escape.

The chickens must've moved out of the road, because we started moving again, slower this time. It wasn't much longer before we stopped and Sleeter opened the door.

"Get out!" he snarled.

The fresh air felt so good as I climbed out of that car! Quint stood close behind Sleeter, both of them ready to catch me if I ran.

I looked around quick enough to glimpse an old blue shack in a dirt yard, surrounded by thick pine trees. I caught a whiff of the ocean and a greasy smell that I thought was gasoline.

"Oh, no you don't!" Sleeter said, tying a rag over my eyes. I yelled and ducked away, clawing at the rag and kicking at him and Quint. Quint yanked my wrists behind my back and marched me toward the front steps. His hands felt as hard and strong as Matthias's, and I knew that there was no escaping him. But I watched enough TV to know that if they took me in their house, nobody would ever see me again.

"HELP!" I screamed. "SOMEBODY, *HELP! I'M NOT HIS NEPHEW* -"

Sleeter clamped his chubby hand over my mouth. "Knock it off, kid, or we'll have to get the *chloroform.*"

Keys jingled and a door opened as they dragged me up the steps. I felt Matthias's big cold hand on my shoulder alongside Sleeter's sweaty one.

"Hush now, Dylan," Matthias whispered. "Be brave. You must pretend to cooperate with them for now. I will not allow them to harm you."

"So, where do ya want him, Mel?" Quint asked as we stepped into the hot and smelly house. "Lock him in my room, or yours?"

"Neither, you dim bulb; he could climb out the windows! Put him in the bathroom, where we can keep an eye on him."

Although Quint didn't let go of me, he pulled off the blindfold and I had a chance to look around before he dragged me down the hall. Their house was almost as gross as their car. Torn shades were pulled down over the windows. I spotted some broken furniture, faded rock band posters on the walls, and even a glowing neon sign that looked like it had come from a bar. Cigarette butts and beer cans and garbage were scattered all over the coffee table and stained carpet. The only clean thing was a huge flat-screened TV that took up one whole wall.

"What *stinks* in here?" I whispered to Matthias.

"That's cigarette smoke." Matthias frowned. "A habit of which I do *not* approve. Now shush."

Quint stuffed me into a dim little bathroom with a tiny window that even I couldn't wiggle through. "Don't worry, kid," he mumbled as he locked the door. "We'll treat ya real good, as long as you do what we say."

I just stared at the door as Quint's footsteps faded down the hall. I couldn't believe that this was happening to me.

"What do we do now?" I asked as I looked up at Matthias.

He shrugged. "We wait for the most opportune time to escape."

"That's *it?* That's all you can think of? Go get help!"

"No. I am not leaving you here alone." He plopped down on the edge of the bathtub and rubbed his forehead. "However, I'm going to have *a lot* of explaining to do, for leaving the light station unattended. If my superiors hear about this..."

I wished that he would just *shut up* about his "superiors!" It was starting to drive me crazy.

I sighed. "Your *superiors* don't know that you left it unattended. You're not going to get in trouble."

Matthias just continued to look at the floor. "Oh, Dylan, I am so sorry that it came to this," he murmured. "I am so ashamed that I could not prevent them from taking you away."

"You *could've* prevented them!" I shouted. "Where *were* you? You could've showed up in front of them, like you did on the island! If they saw you, they would've left me alone and I wouldn't *be* here!"

Matthias sighed. "It is not as easy for me to materialize as you may think. It requires a great deal of energy, and concentration."

"Then how come *I* can see you?" I cried. "I see you all the time!"

He shrugged. "You simply have an ability that few others possess -"

Sleeter yanked the door open and stuck his fat red face in mine, like a drill sergeant.

"Who're you yellin' at, squirt?" he screamed.

Wouldn't you like to know, baldy, I thought. I wanted to tell him that, too. But as I stared into his beady eyes, I was afraid that he would punch me if I talked back to him. I just backed away and looked down at the floor without saying a word.

"*Well?* Answer me when I'm talkin' to you!"

I still couldn't look at him. "I, um…was yelling at Matth… Matthi…" I stammered.

"Well, you better keep your mouth *shut*, boy, or the only way that you'll be getting out of here is in a *hearse!*"

I gasped and looked up at him, and I scooted further into the corner. Sleeter snickered. He seemed pleased that he had been able to scare me.

He turned away and smirked at me over his shoulder. "Spoiled city brat," he muttered as he slammed the door and stomped away.

I sighed and sat on the edge of the bathtub next to Matthias. My legs were shaking. So were my arms. I was glad that Matthias had refused to leave me to find help. I wanted him to stay right here.

"You mustn't make him angry, Dylan," Matthias said.

"What did I do to make him angry? If I wanted to do that, I'd *spit* on him."

Matthias closed his eyes and shook his head. "Dylan, do not even dare. I have already warned you not to provoke him. Do you want him to hurt you?"

I shrugged and looked down at my hands. The grocery list that I had written on my hand was all faded now, but the marker was still in my pocket…

"Matthias! I *got* it!" I dug in my pocket and pulled out my marker. "Go and find me some paper! I'll make a sign for the window so everyone will know where I am!"

Matthias looked over at the tiny window. "I'm not sure that would work, sonny."

"Well, do you have any other ideas?" I snapped.

Matthias frowned at me and faded away. A minute later, a piece of notebook paper slid under the door and Matthias re-appeared, sitting on the edge of the bathtub.

I grabbed the paper off the dirty floor and wrote in my best handwriting. I only had a chance to hold it up in the window for a second, when I heard Sleeter stomping down the hall. "What are you up to now, squirt?" he yelled. "Didn't I tell you to shut up just *five minutes* ago?"

I jumped away from the window and hid the sign behind my back as Sleeter kicked the door open and barged inside.

"Where did you get that paper? What is this?" Sleeter reached around me and snatched away my sign. He held it up and gazed at it with a smirk. *"Help?"* he snickered. "Ain't *nobody* gonna help you, now! The neighbors can't see back here. *Nobody* can!"

He ripped up my sign and held the pieces in front of my eyes, sprinkling them on the floor with a nasty grin.

"You're *really* asking for it, kid. You're gonna force me to use the chloroform, ain'tcha?"

"What's chlor –"

"Shut up!" Sleeter screeched. "Or you'll find out soon enough! Now, sit down and behave yourself while we figure out what to do with you."

He slammed the door and locked it behind him. I just sat on the toilet lid and looked down at the pieces of my sign.

"Matthias?" I whispered. "What's chloroform?"

"It's a dangerous chemical that would render you uncon-scious. Believe me, sonny, you would not want him to use it on you." He straightened up and looked at the door. "I must leave you alone for a little while now, Dylan. I am going out to observe Sleeter and try to discover his plans. If you need me, I can return in seconds. Okay?"

"But *Matthias!* -"

The door rattled on its hinges as Matthias passed through it and into the hall.

I crept to the door and held my breath. I could barely hear Quint and Sleeter talking in the living room. Their low voices drifted down the hall, and I wondered if Matthias was listen-ing as I pressed my ear against the door.

"What if daddy don't give up the lighthouse?" Quint asked. "The kid can't live here the rest of his life."

"Don't worry. I'd find a way to dispose of him. We could take him on a fast boat in the middle of the night, a few miles out to sea, and…you know."

Quint gasped. "Look, Mel, I didn't sign up to murder a kid. We already could do hard time for *this*."

"You're *dumber* than a grapefruit, aren't you? Now, you need to guard the front door! Think you can do *that* much?" Sleeter stomped down the hall, and a door slammed nearby.

Cheers and whistles exploded into the house as someone on TV introduced two wrestlers with funny names. A potato chip bag rattled and a drink can popped open out in the living room. I pictured Quint sprawled out in the tattered recliner, smoking his stupid cigarettes and watching his stupid wres-tling match, not even caring that he had just kidnapped me and locked me in the bathroom.

Matthias came back in, holding a book under his arm. "You were supposed to be *spying*, not *reading!*" I whispered. "You gotta get me out of here! Don't you know that Sleeter wants to *kill* me?"

"Shh! I heard him. But meanwhile, I scouted around and brought you something to pass the time."

He handed me the heavy book. It had a picture of a pirate on the cover. *"Pirates of the Eighteenth Century,"* I read out loud. I started to flip through it and found a chapter on Captain Cutlass.

"I found that in Sleeter's room," Matthias said. "You should see it – books and papers everywhere. He is obviously not a stupid man: his research is very impressive. His room is filled with what appear to be many years worth of handwritten notes, and ceiling-high bookshelves filled with volumes about pirates, treasure hunting, and the history of Maine. But what alarmed me most are his diagrams of the layout of the light station. He is apparently obsessed with finding this treasure."

"Well, what's he doing in there?"

"He is sitting at a desk, staring at a glowing, rectangular screen and tapping his fingers on a platform of buttons, like that of a typewriter."

"That's a computer. Can you go back and see what he's typing?"

"Certainly." Matthias disappeared, and I looked at a painting of Captain Cutlass. He didn't look like much of a pirate; he was all dressed up like George Washington. Even though he held a pistol and sword, he didn't look very scary. Sleeter was scarier than he was. I was afraid that if Sleeter found me reading his book, he might beat me up. I stopped reading and hid it in the cabinet under the sink.

"It's a ransom note," Matthias said as he appeared a moment later. "He's not asking for money – just the deed to the light station."

Beeeeeep!

"Ooh, the pizza's ready!" I heard Quint say to himself as his footsteps headed into the cluttered little kitchen. "And it sure smells good!"

Matthias stood up and moved closer to me when we heard Quint coming down the hall. The key turned in the door. I looked up at Matthias, glad that I wasn't here alone.

Quint opened the door, but he didn't look mad at me, like Sleeter did. Instead, he held out a greasy paper plate. "Here, kid, eat some pizza. You might be here for a while."

I knew that I shouldn't take anything from him, but I was hungry, and the pizza looked good. Then I noticed his long, dirty thumbnail poking into the gooey cheese. One of his hairs had fallen out and lay curled around a blob of anchovies.

I wasn't so hungry once I saw that. Besides, he might've poisoned it. I didn't say anything and pushed the plate away.

Quint looked surprised. "You don't want it? It's really good. It's from Pies on the Point."

"The brat don't need no food, Quint!" Sleeter snarled from his room.

Quint shrugged. "Good. More for me." He grinned and stuffed half the pizza into his mouth, grease running down his stubbly chin as he chewed with his mouth open. The lock clicked as he shut the door behind him.

Matthias looked disgusted. "That is one repulsive young man. And that is a very strange program he is watching. It depicts two costumed fighters who are throwing one another around an arena."

"That's professional wrestling."

"*Wrestling?* That does not resemble any wrestling that *I* have ever seen. But it could work to our advantage, sonny. It will drown out any noise you might make when you escape."

I grinned. *"Really?"*

141

He nodded. "It's really quite simple. I will create a diversion, and unlock your door. Then you will creep down the hall and escape out the front door."

"But *Quint's* out there -"

"Don't worry about Quint! I have a plan. You just need to make your move at *my* command, and not a moment later! Now, I looked around outside, and discovered that we're not far from home! They did all that driving to confuse your sense of direction. There is a motorcar repair shop next door, which also sells gasoline. Does that sound familiar to you?"

"*Yes!* I know just where we are! Dad and I stop there for gas all the time!"

"Good." Matthias nodded. "Then you can find your way home. But you will need to get a good head start on them, before they can get in their motorcar and search for you."

"Can't you just do something to their car?"

He shook his head. "I don't know anything about motorcars. Back in my day, my family had a horse and wagon. Today was the first time that I have ever ridden in a motorcar."

"*Really?*"

He nodded. "Some of the wealthier townsfolk owned those new Model-T Fords that were coming into style. However, *I* could never hope to purchase a motorcar on a paltry *light keeper's* salary."

I shrugged. I couldn't believe that we were talking about *cars* at a time like this. As the wrestling match continued to blare through the house, I imagined Sleeter finishing up with his ransom note and barging into the bathroom to kill me...

Matthias crouched down and put his hands on my shoulders, looking me straight in the eyes. "Are you ready, sonny?"

I took a deep breath and nodded.

"Then we're getting out of here. Now!"

CHAPTER II

The Escape

"Now, when I tell you to move, you mustn't hesitate! Not even if you are frightened," Matthias said as he straightened up. "You must trust me, Dylan. You might not get another chance to escape."

He reached down and plucked some hairs out of my head.

"*Ow!*" I grabbed my head and ducked away from him. "What was *that* for?"

"That is so that when the police investigate your kidnapping, they will find evidence that you were here," he said, sprinkling the hairs around the bathroom. "I've learned much from your father's detective novel. It is a good thing for us that those two don't ever seem to clean this room."

As Matthias faded away, the crowd on TV roared and cheered, and I pictured the wrestlers bouncing off the ropes and leaping on each other. And then...the cheering stopped and little kids' voices sang through the house.

"We love Arlo the Astronaut! Loving each other is what we're taught!"

"Huh?" Quint muttered. *"What* the -"

I snickered. I remembered that I used to love Arlo the Astronaut...when I was in preschool. But now I thought the show was just *weird.* Arlo wasn't even a person; he was a yellow *raccoon* puppet dressed as an astronaut. All of his friends were forest animals dressed as Martians, and they floated through space singing about the alphabet and numbers, and how it was important to share things and help each other. It was for *babies.*

I heard Quint grumbling something until the TV once again blasted the screaming crowd and bellowing wrestlers...

"We're all best friends with Arlo the As-tro-naut!"

"Hey! What's going on with this TV?" Quint whined.

I knew that by then, Arlo and the other animals were holding paws and singing the 'Arlo the Astronaut' song as they danced through outer space.

"What is all this stupid...*c'mon!* I just wanna watch my fight! *AWWWW!"*

What was Matthias doing out there? I wondered. The TV continued to switch back and forth between Arlo and the wrestling, and Quint was getting madder every second.

Ah! I get it, now. Way to go, Matthias! I thought. I jumped when something thumped against the wall, as if Quint had thrown something at the TV.

The key turned in the bathroom lock and Matthias pushed the door open a crack. "Wait for the signal," he whispered.

CRASH! CLATTER! "My *books!* My *research!*" Sleeter shrieked. "My *door!*" He started pounding on his door and twisting the doorknob. "Quint! I'm trapped! Get me out of here!"

"Can't, Mel, I'm fixin' the TV!"

"Dylan!" Matthias shouted. "NOW!"

I yanked the door open and bolted into the hall, then stopped short in the living room when I spotted Quint standing with his back to me, in front of the TV.

"Run!" Matthias cried, shoving me through the living room. "I knocked Sleeter's bookcases over and blocked his door. However, you don't have much time. Never mind what Quint's doing, and run! *Run*, Dylan, and don't stop!"

Quint looked over his shoulder as I headed for the front door.

"Mel, Mel, the kid got out!" he shrieked. He tried to grab me, but tripped over the coffee table and fell on his face.

"You let the kid *escape?*" Sleeter bellowed. "Why, you scrawny runt! Don't let him get away!"

"Home is that way!" Matthias shouted, pointing.

I jumped off the top step and into the dusty yard, fled past the pine trees and the gas station. I didn't stop there to get help. I just ran.

I was almost home when I heard a car speeding up behind me. I looked back. Sleeter and Quint! They were *still* after me!

My sneakers slapped on the dirt road, my own breath loud in my ears as I ran even faster, trying to reach home. It was still so far away.

"Dad!" I screamed. "DAD!"

I looked back again. Quint was driving, revving the engine and swerving all over the road like he was trying to squash me, pebbles spraying out from under the tires. "I'll break your arms, kid!" Sleeter shouted out his window as they went by. They started laughing as they continued down the road.

Where was Dad? I thought.

Quint squealed to a stop, spun around in a cloud of dust, and headed back toward me. "You can't *hide* from *us*, pipsqueak!" he screeched out his window.

I was trapped! I couldn't run into the woods without them seeing me. I waded into the thorny rose bushes beside the road, looking left and right for a place to hide. But there was nothing but the tangled bushes, which snagged my clothes and tore at my arms. It was like trying to walk through a net. I pulled myself away from one big thorn that ripped a hole in my shirt.

"DAAAAD!" I cried, one last time. "*MATTHIAAAAS!*"

I finally ignored my bleeding arms and the thorn bushes, and ducked down into the muddy ditch.

"We got you now, kid!" Quint and Sleeter whooped. They were still laughing at me as the car raced back up the road, louder and closer every second.

Then someone's laughter turned to a shriek. He sounded terrified. "What...*what* the...MEL, *LOOK!*"

I couldn't help it. I peeked up over the edge of the road.

"*Matthias...*" I whispered.

Matthias was standing on the other side of the road, and for the first time...I could *see* through him! He didn't look at me. He just stepped in front of the speeding car and pounded his hands down on the hood, glaring in at Quint. Quint stared back and screamed as the car passed through Matthias, who disappeared in a swirl of white mist.

Quint slammed on the brakes and the car stopped right by my hiding place. He closed his eyes and rested his forehead on the steering wheel, making strange little moaning sounds. His whole body started shaking.

"Quint!" Sleeter bellowed. "What're you *doing*, trying to *kill* us? Learn to *drive*, you moron!"

"Didn't you *see* him?" Quint wailed. "The guy in the blue coat? *I drove right through him!*" Quint hid his face in his hands and began to cry. "That was no man! That was a…a *ghost!* A hideous *ghost!*"

"You idiot!" Sleeter snapped, smacking Quint in the back of the head. "You're useless. Now, stay here. I'm getting out to find that kid."

"Dylan, stay down!" Matthias said as he appeared beside me and sprawled out in the mud, looking like his normal self again. He put his hand on my head and pushed me down on my stomach. My chin scraped against some gravel in the ditch.

"You're hurting me!"

"Sleeter will hurt you a lot worse if he catches you!" Matthias whispered. He did ease up on my head, though, and nodded at a round pipe that ran under the road. "Don't ask questions. Crawl into that culvert and be quiet! It's your only chance."

I did as he told me. The bottom of the pipe was covered with oily water and weird orange mud. I could hear Matthias pushing weeds and brush in front of the opening that I had just crawled through. I knew that he was standing guard at my end of the culvert, so I felt a little safer.

It took forever for them to leave. I couldn't move. I heard Sleeter crashing through the brush, calling me. Quint continued crying in the car. Then Sleeter yelled at him some more, and told him to move over so he could drive.

I heard the car pull away, but didn't dare to make a sound.

"Dylan?" Matthias called. "You okay?"

"Are they gone?" I whispered.

"You're safe, for now. But we need to get you home."

I tried to wiggle back out of the pipe, but couldn't move. "Matthias? I think I'm…I'm *stuck!*"

"Don't worry, m'boy, I'll have you out of there in no time."

He grabbed my ankles and yanked me out of the culvert as if I were a dead fish. My back scraped up against the rough cement. "*Ow!*" I howled. "Take it easy!"

I got to my feet, rubbing my back and blinking in the bright sun. Matthias shook his head. "You're going to have some explaining to do, sonny. You're a mess. Wait until your mother sees you." He reached out and brushed some twigs and leaves off my shoulders. "Now, follow me. I know a shortcut through the woods. We can't stay on this road, in case they come back looking for you."

I looked down at my torn, muddy clothes, bloodstained hands, and scratched-up arms, and the dried brown splotches on my shirt from my bloody nose. My soaked sneakers squished with every step I took. Then I stared at Matthias as I followed him across the road and into the woods. His clothes were spotless. He didn't even have any mud on his shiny black shoes.

He looked over his shoulder at me. "You're going to have to tell your parents what just happened. You know that, don't you?"

"No, way! They would never let me walk to town by myself again. Mom's already really mad at me."

"Why is she mad? You didn't do anything wrong."

"She thinks I lied to her about taking her dish towel, and playing the piano that night. Then she found all of her paintings thrown on the workbench in her studio, and thought that *I* did it! And then she said that I was the one playing with her eggbeater and it left pancake batter on the couch, and she made me clean it up." I glared at him. "Why do you have to play with all of our stuff?"

He shrugged. "I'm a ghost, Dylan. We're naturally curious about the lives and possessions of those who follow us."

"Well, you better put Dad's book back. He's been looking for it."

We didn't say much more as we trudged through the woods. I watched as a chipmunk scampered over the leaves and squatted on its hind legs to nibble at something it held in its paws. It was cute. "Matthias, look," I said, pointing it out.

He hardly glanced at it. "It's just a chipmunk. Now, stop dawdling. Sleeter could be looking for you."

I jogged to catch up with him and stayed close on his heels, until we reached the backyard and headed for the house. Matthias faded away, but I knew he was still around, because the front door opened by itself. I felt his hand on my shoulder, pushing me in the house as Mom hurried into the living room.

"Dylan!" she cried. "Where have you *been?* We were about to go out looking for you!" She stepped back and stared at me. "What on *earth*...look at your *clothes*...you come *right* in this house, young man!" She looked at my scratched-up arms and the dried blood on my shirt. "Oh no, your arms...look at that *blood!* What *happened* to you? Roger! Roger, come here; something has happened to Dylan!"

Mom stared at me. *"Well?"*

I squirmed and looked at the floor. "Um...uh...I, uh...was just exploring on the way home...I walked through this muddy ditch beside the road...and, um...I tried to pick you some of those wild roses, but I got scratched up -"

Matthias poked me in the back. Hard.

"YOW!" I yelped, jumping away and grabbing my sore back. "OK, OK! It was...Quint and Sleeter. They were talking about us in the store...they were chasing me, and they...they *kidnapped* me!"

"Oh, noooo!" Mom wailed. "You were *kidnapped?* Did they hurt you...in *any* way?"

"No, they didn't hurt me, even though Sleeter wanted to take me out to sea and drown me. Quint even gave me some pizza, but I didn't want it." I hadn't wanted to tell Mom and Dad what happened, but once I started, I couldn't stop. "Sleeter wants us to leave so he can tear down the lighthouse and find the treasure...and he *is* the one who slashed the sails – I heard him say so. He wants to...to *shut me up permanently*, he said, because I know too much. They brought me to their house and locked me in the bathroom, but Matthias got me out. Then they chased me down the road in their car, and Matthias made me hide in the culvert 'till they left."

Dad headed for the phone. "That's it. I'm calling the police."

"Dad, no! I'll get in *trouble!*"

"You won't get in any trouble, honey," Mom said, hugging me. "Now, you head straight into that shower and get cleaned up. I'm sure that the officers will want to talk to you."

"Your mother is right, son," Dad said. "Those men are the criminals, not you. And now they're going after *my* family..." Dad looked furious. "They better hope the *police* get to them before *I* do!"

I heard Mom trying to calm Dad down as I went upstairs to the bathroom. She had told me to keep my ruined clothes to show the police, so I tossed them out in the hallway. Then I studied myself in the mirror. There was a long, bloody scrape down my back, from when Matthias pulled me out of the pipe. It was no wonder it hurt so much when he poked me.

When I was done in the shower, I found that someone had left clean clothes on the toilet seat for me. I got dressed, and looked out the window at a police car parked in the driveway. Two cops got out and stepped up on the front porch, where I couldn't see them anymore.

I went downstairs, and one of them introduced himself as the sheriff. The other was one of the cops who came the night that Alondra saw Matthias in her room. I told them what happened, and described Quint and Sleeter. "...They were driving a big, old black car," I said.

"A Buick," Dad added. "From the 1980's."

"I think I know exactly who you're talking about," the sheriff said. "Those two have caused so many problems around here."

"But Matthias helped me get away!" I said. "He *socked* them in the parking lot! And he knocked over Sleeter's bookcases and ruined Quint's wrestling match!"

The sheriff raised his eyebrows. "Matthias?"

Mom looked embarrassed. "That's Dylan's imaginary friend. He thinks that he sees ghosts."

"*Ghosts?*" the other policeman said. He looked around the house and *very* slowly began to creep toward the front door. The sheriff glared at him, but squatted down and looked at me.

"Son, about this Matthias. Does he happen to be a lanky fellow, in a blue suit?"

I nodded, wide-eyed. "That's him!"

"Then your son is telling the truth, ma'am," the sheriff said to Mom. "I've spotted that guy around here several times. Whoever...er...*whatever* he is, he never seems to leave this property."

The cops asked a few more questions and headed back to their car, saying they would call if they heard anything about Quint and Sleeter.

I watched as they pulled away. "*See*, Mom? I *told* you Matthias is real! You *have* to believe the *sheriff!*"

"Dylan, I think you should head up to your room and rest for awhile. You just had a traumatic experience. Your father and I have things to discuss."

She wouldn't take no for an answer. I plodded up the stairs, but I didn't stay in my room. I opened and closed my door to make Mom think I was in there, and then snuck back to the stairway to watch Mom and Dad in the kitchen. I could hear every word that they said as they started talking.

CHAPTER 12

Thunder

"Oh, what have we *done*, Roger? We left the city to have a relaxing vacation and get away from crime and danger, and then this happens? You *promised* me that it would be safe for Dylan to walk to town by himself, and instead, he was *kidnapped!*" Mom stuck her finger in Dad's face. "This is all *your* doing, Roger! *You* brought us here to this...this *place*. I should have *never* agreed to this. I hold you responsible for what happened to Dylan today."

"Well, he made it home safe, and he wasn't hurt, and that's the most important thing. The police are checking into it, and are searching for Quint and Sleeter -"

"And now he's been talking about ghosts, and insists that he sees this...*Matthias* person around the house. He doesn't act like other boys his age. Now he even makes up imaginary friends! Several times, I have seen Dylan staring into space and talking to nothing at all!"

"I wouldn't worry about that, Rorianne," Dad said. "Dylan told me that he was glad we came here, and he doesn't want to go home. He seems so much happier here. And *I* believe that there *is* a ghost; too many strange things have happened around here that can't be explained any other way. You heard the sheriff; even *he* has seen Matthias. I warned you that this place has a reputation."

"Oh, Roger, not you *too!* Do you *really* believe that there is a...a *supernatural creature* in the house?"

"Matthias isn't a *creature*, Rorianne, he's a human being. And Dylan is telling the truth. I took him back to the Historical Society one day, and Mrs. Cooper told us the story of Matthias. He was a real man who had lived and died here. Dylan had found a picture of him, and there's another one of him at the museum. Dylan even found his gravestone in the cemetery, but *you* were *too busy* to take a *moment* to look at it."

Mom folded her arms and glared at Dad. "He may have been a real person, but that doesn't mean that he became a *ghost!* And I don't want Dylan talking to that superstitious woman at the museum. She's a *bad influence* on an impressionable child. It's bad enough that he pretends to talk to some...*invisible man* from the past." She frowned and shook her head. "I think this place has begun to do something to Dylan's mind. I'm going to take him to the doctor if he doesn't stop hallucinating."

Dad sighed. "Do you remember when we moved here, when I said that Uncle Zack always kept Dylan's bedroom door locked? The reason for that was because he knew that it was the haunted room. He told me that he always heard footsteps up there. I just didn't tell Dylan that, because I didn't want to scare him -"

"Roger, sometimes you are just as *exasperating* as your son!"

Mom spun around and marched into their room, and I hustled back up the stairs before she could see me.

I crept back to my room and picked out a library book to read, but I couldn't pay attention to what it said. My room was right above the living room, where I could hear the news on TV. That was more interesting than the book…especially when they started talking about *Sleeter!*

"Police are searching for the suspect wanted for the kidnapping of a ten-year-old boy in Salvation Point, earlier today. The victim escaped unharmed and reported the incident to the police. The suspect, Melvin Sleeter, is described as having a stocky build, shaved head, earrings, and a goatee. Sleeter has an extensive police record and should be considered dangerous.

"His accomplice has already been taken into police custody. Anyone with information on the whereabouts of Melvin Sleeter can contact the Washington County Sheriff's Department at…"

I looked up from my library book as Matthias walked through the closed door. "It's going to be a bad one," he said, as he glanced out the window at the sky.

A hot breeze whistled through the window screen, sending the new white curtains billowing into the room. I pushed them aside and stared across the yard. A line of black clouds had formed far out to sea, even though the sun still shown with a weird yellow light. A swarm of boats headed for the harbor, bouncing across the water as they plowed through the rolling whitecaps.

I stretched out on my bed to read my book, while Matthias sat at the desk and worked on his invisible paperwork. The TV droned on downstairs.

"…Severe thunderstorms are predicted for coastal Maine and all surrounding areas, remnants of the hurricane down south. This is a very dangerous storm system moving through, folks…"

"Roger, I think we should spend the night at a hotel inland." Mom's voice quivered. I could barely hear her above the TV. "The house is so exposed out here; we're surrounded by the sea..."

The phone rang and Dad picked it up before he could answer her. I went back to my book after I realized that I couldn't hear his conversation. I didn't want to risk sneaking down the stairs again.

"Good news!" Dad whooped. "Quint turned himself in. He apparently had a nervous breakdown after Matthias appeared in front of his car -"

"Don't start with this *Matthias* nonsense, Roger. I can't handle it right now."

"Well, this is what the sheriff told me. Quint claimed that he saw a man in blue step out in front of the car before he had a chance to stop. He insisted that he hit him, but felt no collision. The police sent an ambulance to the scene, but couldn't find any sign of a hit-and-run victim."

"But *Sleeter* is still out there?"

"Yes, he is. You know, with all that's going on, I think it's time that we got Dylan his dog. You know, that big Newfoundland that he's always wanted? I would feel better about him roaming around by himself, if he has a big dog to protect him."

"We can't get a *dog*, Roger! We'll be leaving for home in less than a month, and then what would we do with it? I can't picture a big, slobbering Newfoundland in Manhattan."

"Well, I've been thinking. What if we don't go back to the city? What if we move here for good, and -"

"Roger, that is absurd! We can't just pack up and quit our jobs to move to a lighthouse in Maine! And the children -"

"Can get a good education here in Salvation Point," Dad said. "Think about it, Rorianne! There's a good school system here. You can open an art gallery in town, and I can build boats in the winter and teach sailing at the summer camp, like I did when I was younger! It could all work out."

Mom sighed. "Roger, I called Mom and Dad and told them what happened today. They both agreed with me that, for Dylan's safety, we should bring him back to the city first thing tomorrow. He can stay with them until we go back, ourselves."

"No," I muttered.

"You did *what?*" Dad sounded mad. "You made all those plans without discussing it with me first? We're a family. We stay here together as a family. Rorianne, you call them back right now and tell them that Dylan is not going anywhere!"

"It's been settled, Roger. This is the best way to protect him from Sleeter, and maybe when he's back in his normal surroundings, he'll cool it with all this ghost talk. His grandparents are expecting him."

I slammed my book shut and jumped off my bed.

"That's it! I'm *sick* of Mom telling me what to do!"

Matthias didn't even look up from his paperwork. "She's your mother; she has the right to do that."

"I don't care! Now she's mad at Dad for bringing us here, and it's all my fault. I wish she would just go away! I wish that she and Alondra would move back to the city, so Dad and I could stay here by ourselves. She won't listen to anything I tell her! She doesn't care! She thinks I'm stupid to talk about you, but *she's* the stupid one, here! I *hate* her!"

Matthias walked over, grabbed my arm, and shook his finger in my face. "*Look* at me, boy!" he growled. "You need to respect your mother! You must *never* speak ill of her again!"

"But she's so *bossy!* She even tells *Dad* what to do."

"Well, that's not your problem, is it? You will not endear yourself to your mother by throwing a childish tantrum."

"I'm not having a *tantrum*. I'm running away."

Matthias let go of me and raised his eyebrows.

"Actually, I'm *sailing* away," I muttered, as I began stuffing clothes into my backpack. "I'm going back out to Rat Island. I'll build a hut there, and catch fish, and...and..."

Matthias shook his head. "You were raised in the big city, Dylan. You looked like you were scared to death when you were alone in those woods. And you don't know how to survive on an island, by yourself."

"How hard can it be? I've read *Robinson Crusoe*."

"That's a wonderful book, but it's not a manual on survival."

"Then you can come with me, and teach me how. It'll be fun!"

"I cannot stay on any island with you. I belong here at the lighthouse -"

"You *don't* have to stay at the *lighthouse!*" I shouted. "There's no more...*wicks* to trim, or Fresnel lens to dust, or kerosene lamp to clean! And there's no more *logbook* or *paperwork!* The desk is *empty!* Those things are all *gone!* The *lighthouse* doesn't *need* you anymore!"

He looked shocked. "But what would my *superiors* say?"

"Your superiors are all *dead!*" I cried. "And *you're* dead! Why don't you just...just...go to heaven, like a normal person? You just...get me in trouble, and you bug us, and you scare people! You're...*exasperating!* Just...*get lost!*"

Matthias gasped and stared at me, his mouth half open. He looked...betrayed. "A gentleman knows when his presence is not wanted," he whispered. "I apologize for making things difficult for you."

He didn't fade away, the way he usually did. He was gone in a second.

Good! I didn't need *Matthias*, anyway. I didn't need *anybody!*

"And you're not a *gentleman*, either!" I shouted at the empty air.

I grabbed my backpack and tiptoed back down the stairs to the back deck. A gust of wind almost blew the screen door out of my hand.

As I headed for the shed, I looked across the yard at the ocean. The wild gray waves smashed against the rocks and flung spray high into the air. The line of black clouds looked closer than they had before. I had never been out sailing in wind like this, but this was an *emergency!* If I didn't leave now, I would have to go back the city and spend the rest of the summer in Grandma and Grandpa's boring apartment, just watching TV or going to the park. There would be no more sailing, or swimming, or campfires in the backyard. And I wouldn't get to see Matthias until next summer...

Then I remembered that I was mad at him. I didn't care if I ever saw him again! I had thought that he was on my side, and that he would help me run away and learn how to live on the island. But Matthias turned out to be just like every other grown-up I knew. I couldn't believe that I ever thought he was my friend!

I yanked open the shed door and grabbed my fishing pole. Everyone's life jackets hung on the wall next to Dad's boat stuff, but I left mine there and shut the door. I didn't have to follow Dad's dumb life jacket rule anymore! I didn't have to follow *anyone's* rules!

The wind blew my hair into my eyes as I stomped down the road, scowling at the wild roses that rustled along the shore. I didn't think about how much I had wanted to go home just a few hours ago. Now I just wanted to get *away*.

When I passed the tire marks in the road where Quint had spun around and stopped, I remembered how Matthias had made me crawl into the culvert. That had probably saved my life, but I didn't care about all that anymore. I figured that I was safe from Sleeter, now. He was probably hiding out until the cops give up looking for him.

A burst of chilly air whooshed against my back as I heard Matthias's shoes plodding along behind me. I groaned. I thought that I had gotten rid of him!

"I know you're there!" I yelled. "I can hear your footsteps."

Matthias appeared and grabbed my shoulder. Not too gently, either. "Dylan, think about what you're doing." His voice rumbled like the low thunder that I heard across the bay. "You just barely escaped from Sleeter today. He's still out there, and looking for you."

"I don't *care* about Sleeter anymore!" I snarled, tugging his hand off my shoulder. "Dad told us that we can't let him scare us away, and ruin our summer here."

"You also forgot your life vest. You know that you can't go in the boat without your -"

"GO...AWAY!"

But Matthias didn't go away. He walked beside me and wouldn't shut up.

"You know, your parents haven't discovered that you've snuck out of the house, yet. If you turn around and go home right now, they'll never find out."

"I told you, I'm not going back!"

He sighed. "What if I told you that your parents have a great surprise for you? It's something that you're really going to like."

"What? They're getting me a *dog?*" I shrugged. "I don't care about getting a dog anymore. I just want to stay here."

"Dylan, do you *really* think that your parents would allow you to stay here after you've run away from home? And do you think that the ranger would allow you to stay on the island if he found you?"

"He's not going to find me. I'll hide in the woods. But if he does, I'll just…sail away."

Matthias grabbed my arms and yanked me so close to him that our noses almost touched. "You think you're a *real* sailor, eh?" he shouted, giving me a hard shake. "Well, let me tell you something, boy: you're not a real sailor; you're a little fool. A *real* seaman wouldn't risk his life and his boat in a storm like this, if it wasn't necessary."

"It's necessary!" I snapped. "I don't want to go back to the city." I pushed him away and tore down the road toward the harbor.

"DYLAN!" Matthias bellowed. I left him standing in the middle of the road, staring at me with his hands on his hips, but I knew that he wouldn't stay there for long.

Small-craft warning flags flapped in the wind as I sprinted into the harbor with Matthias close behind me. The lobster boats all bobbed and pulled at their moorings, as if they were trying to escape from the storm.

I stalked down the dock past *Rorianne Rose*, and found *Thunder* bucking in the waves that smacked her sides. Fat raindrops splattered the dock as I fought to untie the rocking boat, which jerked the rope tight with every wave.

Matthias popped up beside me and pointed at the black sky. "I don't like the looks of those clouds over there, boy. Those are thunderheads. See how high and dark they are? I predict that the storm will hit within ten minutes."

"How do *you* know that? You're not a weatherman."

Matthias sighed. "Dylan, I have lived beside the sea my entire life and death. I have seen many a storm hit, and many a ship founder on the rocks. This storm is not the first."

"But this is just rain. I'll be on the island when the storm starts."

He shook his head. "You are making a very poor decision, and a very big mistake."

We both looked up as the rain pounded the dock and swept sheets of water flying through the air. In seconds, I was as soaked as I would have been if I had jumped off the dock, but the raindrops rolled off Matthias without getting him wet. Amazed, I reached out and touched his dry coat, as the water trickled into my eyes and my drenched T-shirt clung to my back.

"See? This is why you can't go out there!" he said. "This rain is only the beginning."

"It's only water! I'll dry out!"

Matthias folded his arms and scowled down at me. "You know, I can physically restrain you, and prevent you from doing this."

"Then why don't you?" I dropped my backpack and fishing pole into the boat and glared at him.

He shrugged. "Because you're old enough to make your own decisions. And this is one of them."

I took the oars out from under the seat and jammed them down into the oarlocks. Matthias touched my arm. "It's not too late to change your mind, sonny," he said, with a sad smile. I knew that he was worried about me.

"No." I shook my head and climbed into the boat. "I...I have to go."

I knew that I had hurt his feelings when I yelled at him back in my room, but I didn't have time to think about that. I rowed *Thunder* through the maze of lobster boats, until I reached the open water where I could start to sail.

I looked through the rain and saw Matthias standing on the dock watching me leave. "Stay away from the cliffs!" he shouted.

Then he slowly turned away and disappeared.

***

As the rain pelted *Thunder's* wooden deck, I spotted the black hill of Rat Island three miles away. At least, I thought it was the island. I raised the sail and aimed *Thunder* to the northeast, wishing that I had brought along a compass.

And I was starting to wish that I stayed home.

I had already tipped over three times. The wind had slammed the sail back and forth, the boom just missing my head before capsizing the boat again. Each time, it got harder to pull *Thunder* upright, as the water poured back over the sides and the soaked sail pulled the mast under the waves.

I turned *Thunder* so that the wind blew against her side, and moved up onto the seat. *Thunder* tore along, almost sideways through the water while I tried not to fall over backwards into the bay. The cold salt water splashed over the seat, soaked my jeans and stung my scratched-up arms and back. I hooked my legs under the seat and held on tight to the tiller. It felt like a living thing as it tried to yank itself out of my hand.

I remembered what Dad had told me the day we went to the island. *It's three miles out to sea*, he said. *It can get too rough out there for a little boat like* Thunder...

He had been right, but it was too late to turn back, now. The waves flung *Thunder* way, way, *way* up until her bow pointed almost to the sky. As I looked up into the rolling clouds, I thought the boat would fall over backwards on top of me! Then my stomach lurched into my throat when *Thunder* crashed back down, like she was diving straight to the bottom of the sea. The foamy black water broke over the bow and splashed over my head, but *Thunder* always popped back up... and it started all over again. It was like a bad carnival ride that I thought would never end.

My dripping clothes clung to me. My hands had gone numb and stiff as I held on, shivering, to the seat. I was so cold, but knew that since the rain wasn't going to stop, I couldn't stop, either. Not until I got to the island.

Matthias's sleeve brushed against my arm as he appeared next to me.

"Ease up on that mainsheet a bit, sonny, and spill some of this wind. You're heeling over too much."

"*Matthias!* What are you *doing* here? I thought you had to stay at the lighthouse!"

"No, I've been here in the boat with you the whole time. Did you really think I would leave you out here alone? And *don't* let her jibe! The boom could knock you overboard. I'm trying to keep you from getting *killed*."

"You mean from the storm?"

"No. Look over there. We have...company." He pointed at an old motorboat, bouncing over the waves as it sped toward us. A bald-headed man sat back in the stern, shouting something over the roar of the huge outboard motor. Then he drove straight at me.

"*Sleeter!*" I yelped.

I was sailing *Thunder* harder than I ever had before. I couldn't go any faster. The spray splashed up over the bow and into my eyes. I tried to wipe it away until *Thunder* bounced up and down on the waves, almost throwing me off the seat.

I squinted through the rain, searching for that black shape that I had thought was the island. All I spotted was the lighthouse beam circling through the sky, getting closer and closer, while the wind tried to push *Thunder* into the sea.

"I can't hold it down! I'm not heavy enough!" I cried.

"Well, I can't help you there. I'm weightless," Matthias snapped. "You should've thought of that before you got yourself into this mess."

"But the cliff! He's chasing us into the cliff!"

Matthias watched as Sleeter drove alongside us, laughing and shouting at me.

"I'll be right back," Matthias said, disappearing before I could answer. He reappeared in the motorboat and yanked the controls out of Sleeter's hand.

Sleeter's boat swerved left and dumped him into the waves. I thought that was the end of him, but he came back up, sputtering and swimming toward *Thunder*. The waves broke over his head, but he swam fast and strong, glaring up at us whenever he could.

Matthias reappeared beside me and we watched as the motorboat zoomed off toward the cliffs by itself. CRUNCH! I winced as the empty boat slammed into the rocks, its bow crumpled. Water poured inside until the waves threw the crushed boat into the air. It flipped end-over-end, its propeller still spinning before the boat came down engine-first. In seconds, it was gone.

Thunder *could be next!* I thought, tightening my hold on the tiller. I looked from the spot where the motorboat sank, and back to Sleeter. He was trying to grab *Thunder's* rudder!

I screamed and shrank back against Matthias. He was the only help I had now, but he looked as scared as I was.

Matthias put his arm around me. "*Don't* panic, sonny," he said. I was surprised at how calm he sounded, because he sure didn't look that way. He stared at the cliffs, his mouth tight and trembling. "I won't let anything happen to you. Just trust me."

"But Sleeter's..." I gulped and shook my head, staring. Sleeter was climbing into the boat! We were going to tip over! I almost tumbled off the seat as *Thunder* bounced up and down on the waves and water gushed over the side.

Matthias let go of me. "Release the mainsheet and tiller, boy," he ordered.

"*What?* Are you crazy?" I wasn't sure if I should listen to him. After all, he had crashed his father's fishing boat...

"I said, let the boat on her own! *Now*, before we capsize!"

There was nothing more I could do. Matthias nodded as I opened my hands, letting the sail blow out of control, the tiller swinging away from me. But Matthias was right. As soon as I let go, *Thunder* swung around and faced into the wind. The bouncing stopped and the mast popped back upright. But now Sleeter crouched in the corner, grinning at me like one of Cutlass's pirates. "You might as well give it up, kid!" he snarled. "I always finish what I start!"

I scrambled up onto *Thunder's* flat front deck, staring at Sleeter and clutching the mast to keep from sliding off.

"Don't be afraid," Matthias told me.

He dissolved into a glowing white mist that surrounded Sleeter like fog. Sleeter shrieked and started jumping around, rocking the boat and swatting at the mist like it was a swarm of bugs. The mist swirled around and formed into the shape of Matthias, who shoved Sleeter off his feet.

"Sit down in the boat!" Matthias shouted. Sleeter gasped.

"Who are you? What...*what* are you?" he stammered. He tried to crawl away, but the misty form of Matthias grabbed him and pinned him against the boat.

"You don't *know* me, Sleeter? I'm the *old, dead lighthouse keeper* that you said you're not afraid of. And you don't learn, do you?"

Sleeter shrieked. "Get *away* from me, you...you *freak!* You *monster!* Leave me *alone!*" He tried to jump overboard, but Matthias wouldn't let him go.

Sleeter hid his face in his hands and shook his head. "I don't believe in ghosts," he whimpered. "Ghosts don't exist! I don't believe in -"

"You *don't* believe in *ghosts?*" Matthias bellowed as he yanked Sleeter's hands away and changed back into his solid form. "*Look* at me!"

Sleeter panicked. He broke away from Matthias and lunged at me, grabbed my ankle and pulled me toward him. "MATTHIAS!" I screamed.

Matthias pulled an oar from under the seat and swung it at Sleeter's head like a baseball bat.

CRACK!

The oar connected with Sleeter's head and his hand slid off my ankle. He fell facedown on the floorboards, eyes closed.

Matthias looked at me. "What do you say we head back to the harbor, huh?" He set his foot on the unconscious Sleeter's back. "I'll watch him. *He's* not going *anywhere*...except to jail."

I knew that I was in trouble. I was afraid to go home and face Mom and Dad, but was even more afraid of the storm. I didn't want *Thunder* to end up like Sleeter's motorboat, so I slid down onto the seat and picked up the tiller...

"DYLAN! LOOK OUT!" Matthias cried.

Last thing I saw was the boom swinging towards my head, smacking me in the face. I toppled overboard and sank beneath the waves.

CHAPTER 13

Home

When I woke up, I thought that I was still out in the storm. The thunder boomed and crackled and rain pounded above my head, but I wasn't struggling in the cold ocean anymore. Did it all really happen? Sleeter and Quint...the culvert...*Thunder* and the cliffs and the sinking motorboat...the whole day just seemed like a bad dream.

I moved my scratched-up arms, and felt warm and dry pajamas covering them. *Who put these on me?* I wondered, as I lay under the heavy blankets that were tucked up around my shoulders. I was back in my squeaky old bed with the sagging spot in the middle, and it never felt more comfortable. I was so tired.

I opened my eyes and looked across the room. Mom and Dad were there, watching me, Mom in the desk chair and Dad in the big leather one near my bed.

"Dylan?" Mom cried. "Oh, thank *goodness!*" She jumped up and rushed over to my bed, hugging me through my blankets. Her eyes were all red and puffy, like she'd been crying.

"You've been unconscious for awhile," Dad said. "You have a bad concussion. We tried to take you to the emergency room, but found that there were trees down all over the roads." He held up a baggie of melting ice cubes. "We've been icing your head. It's kept the swelling down, but I bet you're going to have quite an impressive bruise tomorrow."

Mom sat beside me on my bed, frowning down at me. "You are in big trouble, young man," she said. It sounded like she might start crying again. "*Big* trouble!"

"Yeah, I know. You're shipping me back home first thing in the morning, right?"

Mom and Dad glanced at each other. "You just stay in bed and rest, for now," Dad said. "We'll discuss it in the morning. We have a lot to talk about."

"Your father is right, young man. You need to think about what you just did today."

Dad walked over and laid the ice back on my forehead. "It was the boom, wasn't it?"

I nodded. "The boom hit me in the head. And then I was in the water. I couldn't breathe." I looked at Dad. "Somebody pulled me out. I thought it was you."

Dad stared at me for a moment, and then looked at Mom. "Honey, I'd like to talk to him now...alone."

"What's this all about?"

Dad frowned at her. "It's *man* talk."

Mom shrugged and walked out the door.

"Dylan!" Dad said in a low voice. He glanced at the door to make sure Mom was out of sight. "It was Matthias. I *saw* him. He had rescued you from the storm, and brought you back home. He was standing on the front porch with you in his arms. If it weren't for him, you would've drowned."

"You *saw* him?"

"Yes. I recognized him from the picture at the museum. He was wearing that old-fashioned uniform, and his skin was ice-cold. But the strangest thing was that, even though you had both been in the ocean and rain, his clothes and hair were dry."

"Did you talk to him?"

"He didn't say a word. He just handed you to me, and when I looked toward him again, he was gone."

"Does Mom know?"

"I didn't tell her a thing. And neither will you...*will* you, Dylan?"

"I guess not."

"You *better* not. You know how much that subject upsets your mother. And another thing! That was a rotten way for you to talk to Matthias today, after he was your pal all summer."

"What do you mean?"

"I believe that I overheard you telling him to *get lost*, among other things. And after he had saved you from Sleeter and Quint today! I think you owe him an apology."

"I know." I nodded and closed my eyes. "Dad? Is Mom still taking me back to Grandma and Grandpa's tomorrow? If she is, I don't want to go."

"I told you that we'd talk about that in the morning. Good night, Dylan." He shut the door and left me alone in my dark room.

Matthias appeared after Dad left. As the lighthouse beam swung across the walls, I spotted him sitting at the desk and scribbling something with a frown.

"Are you writing in your logbook again?" I asked, turning on my bedside lamp.

"Yes. I'm writing about the dumb kid that I just had to rescue because he wouldn't listen to what anyone told him."

"Um...sorry..." I snuck a look at his angry face, and wished I hadn't.

"Sorry? *Sorry?* You *should* be sorry, boy. And you should be *ashamed* of yourself. Your parents were frantic. You could've been killed."

Matthias stood up and jabbed his finger at me. "You have a *lot* to learn about the sea, boy. You had *no* business being out there today. If you're so arrogant that you think you can sail that little boat in a storm, then you don't deserve to even have it."

"But -"

"Dylan, at one time, you told me that your boat was your most prized possession. What made it even more special was that your father built it for you. Now, tell me: was this any kind of a way to treat your *prized possession?* It might very well be destroyed on those rocks right now, and for what reason? All for *nothing*, that's what. All because you acted like a *spoiled* and *immature* little brat who -"

"I *know!*" I wailed. "That's the worst part of it. Dad built it for me, and now it's probably wrecked. I feel bad enough about it already. Don't make me feel worse."

He looked at the floor and began to speak in a softer voice. "I guess you already know that I lost my father to those very cliffs. I didn't want to lose you, too."

"Matthias? How did...um...your father...you know...*die?*"

Matthias looked out the window, standing with his back to me. When he began talking, I could barely hear him above the rain. "It was in a storm a lot like this one. Our boat had crashed into the cliffs, and was starting to sink. My father had gotten tangled in the rigging, and was being pulled underwater. He drowned before I could free him." He shuddered. "When I saw Sleeter's boat go down, I felt like I was watching it happen all over again."

"Matthias?" I mumbled. "I'm, um…I'm sorry I was rude. And I'm glad you didn't get lost."

I looked up at him when he didn't answer me. For some reason, he looked very serious.

"Look, sonny, there's something that I need to tell you. I might be leaving soon."

"*Leaving?* What do you mean? You *live* here."

"But this isn't my *home*, Dylan. This earth hasn't really been my home since I died. It's made for you mortals, not us spirits." He sighed. "You should be happy for me, sonny. I could cross over at any time. I just wanted to prepare you, in case I don't get a chance to say goodbye."

He pulled my blankets up around my shoulders. "Go to sleep. It's been a long day today, and you need your rest. I have to get out to the lighthouse; there's a lot of work to do tonight."

"Will you…still be here tomorrow?"

"I might be. But I can't promise you that. Whatever happens will be for the best."

I watched as Matthias floated through the window and disappeared into the rain. I wondered if I'd see him again.

Matthias was just as much a part of my life here, as the lighthouse, *Thunder*, and Salvation Point, and even the buried pirate treasure. It wouldn't be the same without him.

I guess that it really didn't matter. I knew that this was my last night in Maine. Mom was going to make me pack up and leave for Grandma and Grandpa's house in the morning.

I rolled over. Hot tears began to run down my face and soak into my pillow, but I didn't try to stop them. I continued to cry until someone tapped on my door.

"Dylan? May I come in?"

Alondra!

I sighed. I just wanted to be left *alone*. "If you want, I guess."

I wiped my eyes on my sheet and tried to stop sniffling. I couldn't let her see me crying, so she'd have another reason to laugh at me. But I couldn't stop.

"Dylan? What's wrong?" she said in a soft voice.

I sat up and glared at her. "Everything. *Everything's* wrong! Matthias is leaving...and now, so am I! You know that Mom's sending me back home, right? That was why I ran away...but I even ruined that." I started crying even harder. Just like a *baby*. I was so embarrassed.

Alondra...actually reached out and...*hugged* me. I don't remember her *ever* hugging me.

"Shhh...Dylan, it'll be okay," she whispered. "Now, lay back down. You're hurt."

Alondra sighed. "Look, I came in here because...I have a confession to make, and I had wanted to tell you as soon as it happened, but I...I just couldn't."

"Oh, yeah?" I tried to sound tough.

"*Yeah.* I never told Mom or Dad this...but do you remember when we were in the museum, and we saw that picture of the grumpy-looking man in the hat? Well, he was the man I saw in my room. Mr. MacMurray...*Matthias.* The...the...*ghost.*"

"So you believed in him all this *time?* Then *why* did you keep on making *fun* of me about him?"

"I don't *know!* I just thought that...if I refused to believe that there was a *ghost* in the house, he would just...go away. But sometimes at night, I could hear you talking to someone in here. I wanted so hard to believe that you were just talking to yourself. But…Matthias was in here with you the whole time, wasn't he? And you were actually…*talking* to him?"

"Sure." I sniffled and nodded. "Matthias is cool. If you don't freak out about him, you can talk to him, too."

Alondra held up her hands. "OK, I'm not *that* comfortable with him. *Normal* people don't like ghosts. You're supposed to be *afraid* of them."

I shrugged. "They're nothing to be afraid of. They're just people."

She closed her eyes and shuddered. "*Dead* people. But seriously, Dylan, I…I just wanted to tell you that I'm sorry for the way I treated you all summer."

I stared at her. "Oh. Right."

"Dylan, you're not being fair!"

"Why should I be? You're not sorry! I bet you're *happy* that I'm leaving tomorrow. I know how much you hate it here, and how much you hate *me!*"

Alondra gasped. "You really think that I *hate* you? I don't hate you, Dylan; you're my little brother! You could've *died* out there today!"

She sighed. "Listen. I know that I've been a total brat all summer. I gave you and Mom and Dad such a hard time about staying here. But you know, deep down…once I got used to living in a haunted house in the middle of nowhere, I think it's really been kind of an awesome summer. I don't think I'll ever become a…*small-town* kind of a girl, but I suppose that if we're *really* going to be coming up here every year, now…I think I can handle it."

"Yeah? Well, I bet you wish that Mom was taking *you* home tomorrow, instead of me."

"Look, Dylan, Mom's not...never mind. They'll tell you what's going on in the morning."

I wondered what Alondra meant, but didn't have time to think about it. Soon after she left, I finally fell into a dark, dreamless sleep.

***

CRACK! CRASH...RUMBLE...

I sat up in bed and stared into the dark. What *was* that? Was the *lighthouse* hit by lightning? Did it fall down in the storm? I jumped out of bed and looked out the window. It wasn't the lighthouse. Its beam still circled around and shone through the rain and fog. I spotted Matthias's shadow moving around in the lantern room.

The door slammed downstairs, and the porch light came on. Dad ran through the yard, and stopped near the edge of the cliff. He fell to his knees and began pawing at the ground, then threw his arms into the air and whooped.

I wanted to see what was going on, but got too dizzy to stand. I wobbled back to bed and tried to stay awake, listening as much as I could. The front door opened, and Mom and Dad scurried around and talked in low voices. "...Honey, *honey*, get a flashlight," Dad said. "No, the big one. And I need to go get a shovel..."

CHAPTER 14

A New Beginning

My room was bright and sunny when I woke up the next morning. The new white curtain flapped around in the breeze that came in the open window. It was the beginning of another day of my summer vacation at the lighthouse...

No, it wasn't. I remembered Mom and Dad's argument, and that Mom was sending me back home to New York.

"Good morning, Dylan," Dad said. Startled, I looked over at him and Mom. They were sitting in their chairs again, watching me. It was like they were waiting for me to wake up, like they did last night.

"Morning," I mumbled.

"Dylan, I imagine that you know why we're in here right now," Dad said. "We need to talk about your little...adventure yesterday."

"*Adventure?* Roger, that wasn't an *adventure*, he ran away from *home!*"

I sighed. "I know what you're going to tell me. I already got a lecture from Matthias."

Mom folded her arms. "And *now*, you're going to get one from *us.*"

"Can I go to the bathroom first?" I asked.

Dad shrugged. "Just don't go downstairs, okay? There's something down there that I don't want you to see right now. It's a surprise. No peeking!"

I wondered what kind of a surprise it was as I went down the hall to the bathroom. Matthias had said that they had a surprise for me, when we were on the way to the harbor yesterday. It was something that I would really like, he said. A *dog?* But what was the point of getting a dog, if I was going home? Maybe it had something to do with that huge crash that I heard outside last night. That was the loudest sound that I had ever heard in my life.

I looked in the bathroom mirror and studied the big purple bruise on my forehead. It was still swollen and sore, and it made my head hurt.

Mom and Dad were waiting for me when I went back to my room. They made me sit on my bed, and told me all the same things that Matthias did last night. Then Dad talked on and on about responsibility, and he told me how disappointed he was in me.

I was glad that he didn't mention my missing boat.

Matthias appeared in the doorway just as Dad was telling me that he hoped I learned my lesson. I was happy that Matthias was still here, but what was going to happen to *me?*

"…Dylan, there's something else that we need to tell you," Dad said. "Your mother and I have been talking, and we agreed -"

"*Against* my better judgment," Mom broke in.

"…that we're all going to remain here in Salvation Point."

"*Really?* We get to *live* here? For *good?*"

"*Well…*" Dad said. "I've convinced your mother to give it *one* year to see how it goes. If it all works out, next year we'll make a final decision to see if we stay here permanently. But this doesn't mean that you're not still in *big* trouble!"

"Matthias, did you hear that? We're not going back to the city! I can stay here with you! It's gonna be great!" I jumped up and threw my arms around his cold body. I remembered how I had been afraid of him at the beginning of the summer. That seemed like so long ago.

Matthias patted my back. "I heard, sonny. And I'm very happy for you. I know how much you love it here."

"But that's not all," Dad said, smiling. "I have something to show you. Come on downstairs."

Matthias faded away, but I heard his footsteps on the stairs behind us as we headed down to the kitchen.

"So, what does Alondra think of staying here?" I asked. "I bet she was mad."

Mom shrugged. "She wasn't happy, but she handled it better than we thought."

I was amazed at how everything was working out. But nothing was more amazing than what I found on the kitchen table…

A wet piece of canvas covered the table, hiding…something *big*. Mom and Dad stood back and nodded, smiling, as I lifted the canvas and stared.

Gold coins and colorful jewels glinted in the light. A pile of rusty old flintlock pistols and fancy swords took up one whole end of the table.

"No, *way*," I whispered. "The treasure...it *has* to be. Captain Cutlass's treasure..."

"A piece of the cliff had broken off during the storm," Dad said. "It had been hit by lightning, and slid into the sea. This had been underneath the rocks for hundreds of years."

"What *is* all this?" I ran my fingers through the pile of muddy old coins. "*Gold?* Real *gold?*"

"It looks like it. And those weapons and jewelry must be worth a fortune. Your mother and I were up all night, bringing it in the house. I hope we didn't miss anything."

I looked over and saw Matthias leaning against the wall, watching Dad and me. "Matthias, come here. You've *got* to see this. It wasn't just a story. It was really true!" I looked at Dad with a big grin. "We're *rich!*"

"We'll see," Mom said, as she and Dad looked at each other. They didn't notice that some of the coins seemed to float in mid-air when Matthias picked them up to look at them. He looked astonished.

"Dylan, we need to keep quiet about this, for now," Dad said. "It's very important that you and your sister do *not* mention this to *anyone*. I'm putting it in the closet until -"

The phone rang. "Honey, it's for you," Mom said.

"Hello? Yes, this is Roger Flint...you *did?* Oh, my son will be so glad to hear it! I'll be over right away to pick it up. Thanks for calling."

Dad hung up and looked over at me. "Dylan, someone found your boat washed up on the shore."

"*Really?*" I started to smile. "It's not *wrecked?* It's okay?"

"Well, they said that she's a little banged up, but looks fixable. And guess what: *Sleeter* was passed out inside!"

"That's because...I think I remember...Sleeter grabbed me. Matthias whacked him with the oar, and knocked him out."

Dad frowned. "Sleeter *grabbed* you? Well, then it's a good thing Matthias was with you. There's no telling what might've happened if you were alone. Lucky for Sleeter, the boat never capsized. Anyway, the people called the cops, and he's in jail. We don't have to worry about him anymore."

After lunch, Dad hauled *Thunder* home and put her in the shed. "You're not taking your boat out again this summer, Dylan," he told me as he padlocked the door. "And next year, you will not go out sailing unless I'm there to keep an eye on you. Remember what we talked about before? You showed me that you're not responsible enough to have your own boat."

"But *Dad!*"

Dad looked down at me. "Dylan, what was the most important rule that I ever taught you about your boat?"

"To always wear a life jacket."

"Yes. And what did I tell you when we first came here?"

I sighed. "To stay away from the cliffs."

"*Exactly.* And you broke *both* of those rules."

"But *Sleeter* was chasing me towards -"

"Sleeter would not have been chasing you if you had not been out there to begin with."

I sighed again and slumped along behind Dad as he headed back toward the house. I'd only get in more trouble if I argued with him, but I couldn't resist complaining to Matthias, who had appeared beside me.

Matthias didn't look sympathetic. "It's your own fault, boy," he said with a shrug. "If you had only listened to me when you were running off yesterday, then this could've all been avoided. I was about to tell you that you were going to stay here for good. But you wouldn't listen, and look what happened! I've never seen a child as *stubborn* and *pigheaded* as you."

"I'm *not* stubborn, and – Dad! Look!" I pointed at a big white pickup truck that was speeding up the road. "Look how fast they're driving!"

I glimpsed a logo on the truck as it passed Dad, Matthias, and me and stopped at the lighthouse. "That's the Coast Guard," Dad said as he headed for the truck. I followed along behind him. "I wonder what's going on?"

Two men in uniforms jumped out and unlocked the lighthouse door. "Mr. Flint, we received a message that the equipment in the lighthouse was malfunctioning," the older one of them said. "The light had gone out during the storm!"

"Yes, we would've been here sooner, but the storm knocked down several trees across the road."

Dad stared at them. "I've been awake all night long, and I can assure you, that the light had been on."

"But that's *impossible!*" the older man said.

The younger one looked at him. "It's not so impossible if you believe the old stories about this place. There's said to be a phantom lighthouse keeper..."

The other man just glared at him and shook his head as they disappeared into the lighthouse.

Mom took the car and drove to town to "just run an errand." Meanwhile, I helped Dad as he started pulling some weeds out of a new flowerbed that he had planted below the lighthouse. It didn't really need it, though. I knew that Dad was just waiting there to talk to the Coast Guard men and find out what was wrong.

When they finally came back outside, they told Dad that one of the machines in the lighthouse top had broken, and they replaced it with another one that they had brought in the truck. The old man still didn't believe Dad when he told him the light never went out, but *I* knew what...or *who*...really kept it lit last night. I think Dad did, too.

***

As the Coast Guard men took off back down the road, Mom pulled in and started unloading grocery bags from the car. "What's all this?" Alondra asked.

"It's some sodas and ice cream cake for our celebration," Dad said with a big grin. "Today's a special day. It's the first day of our new life here."

"For a *year*, Roger. A *year*," Mom said. But her smile was almost as big as Dad's. "Now kids, help me get this in the house. You'll need to get some plates and spoons...and some ice for your drinks."

"Hey, how 'bout we all eat at the top of the lighthouse?" Dad asked.

Mom frowned. "Roger, what on earth for?"

"Well, if we're going to *live* at the light station, don't you think it's fitting that we *celebrate* at the top of the *lighthouse?*"

Alondra rolled her eyes. "Dad, you are *so* corny!" But she actually *smiled* and took a plate of ice cream cake without complaining.

We all carried our plates of cake to the top of the lighthouse, where we ate on the balcony...I mean, the *gallery*...below the lantern room. "We can't spill any ice cream up here," I told everyone. "Matthias cleans the lighthouse every day. He would be mad if we make a mess." Mom frowned and shook her head, but didn't say anything.

It wasn't a *celebration*, really. We just ate our cakes and looked out at the scenery while we talked about what we wanted to do now that we're staying here for the year. I wondered if Matthias was listening to us, but I only saw him for a second. He was standing at the railing looking out to sea, as if he thought he would never see it again.

All of us – even Alondra – kept talking and laughing as we started back down the lighthouse stairs with our empty plates, which were sticky with melted ice cream.

I looked up when I heard footsteps just ahead, and then spotted Matthias walking down the stairs.

"Matthias, wait," I said. He stopped and looked over his shoulder at us.

Alondra shrieked and stumbled up the stairs to hide behind Dad. Mom gasped and grabbed Dad's arm. "Roger? *Who* is... *what* is...could that really be...*Matthias? No*...it *can't* be...that's *impossible!*"

Dad nodded. "Dylan was telling us the truth the entire summer, Rorianne, and you refused to believe him."

Mom looked like she was going to pass out. Dad put his arm around her waist to keep her from falling down the stairs. "Matthias?" she whispered.

"Ma'am?"

"I...I want to apologize for not believing in you. Thank you for taking care of my son. You saved his life."

He shrugged. "I was just doing my job, ma'am."

Matthias smiled and held his hand out to me. I walked down the three steps that separated us. I knew what was coming.

"It's time for you to leave now, isn't it?" I said in a small voice.

Matthias nodded. "Yes, Dylan...it's time."

"But...but you *have* to stay to take care of the lighthouse! Remember when you told me that if you didn't, the sailors could die?"

"I'm leaving it in good hands. You and your family are the ones who belong here now. I told you that this place gets in your blood...and that's exactly what happened to you."

"I wish you didn't have to leave." I looked down at my feet, until I felt his icy fingers under my chin, tilting my face up to look at him.

"Hey, don't be sad. It's a new beginning, Dylan," he said softly. "It's a new beginning for *both* of us. But it isn't the end. We'll meet again someday."

"When?"

"I don't know. That's not up to us. But in the meantime, remember to behave for your mother. And from now on, stay away from those cliffs!"

"I'll remember. And I'll take good care of the lighthouse for you. I promise."

He smiled and patted my shoulder. "You're going to be alright, sonny."

"Will I...ever see you again?"

He shook his head. "Not on this earth. My work here is done."

Matthias gave me a hug and sent me back up the stairs to join my family. Then he smiled at me, and vanished into the air where he had stood.

Epilogue

"I can't believe that you actually...*hugged* him," Alondra said, shuddering, as we left the dim lighthouse for the sunny backyard. "What does he...you know, *feel* like?"

I shrugged. "He feels just like us. Except cold."

"Alondra," Mom called her over and talked to her in a low voice, but I heard anyway. "Please don't bother your brother right now. He's just lost his friend."

I trudged back to the house behind everyone else. Matthias wasn't *lost*, I told myself. I knew where he was; I just couldn't see him now. And he *did* tell me that we would meet again, but maybe it wouldn't be until after I died, myself. It was too sad to think about.

I finally understood why his work on earth was done. Although he couldn't save his father from the shipwreck, he saved me. He even kept the lighthouse lit after the modern equipment broke down. Still, I expected him to show up in my room that night so we could talk. But he didn't come back that night, or the next. Now all that I had of him were his binoculars and compass, and the old picture of him and his father on the boat. Dad put it in a frame and hung it on my wall so I'd see it every day.

Our house was a lot quieter now. It felt...empty. There was no more midnight piano playing, or footsteps upstairs, or missing objects, or cold spots in the house. Alondra finally took the portraits out of her room, and never had another problem with them. That was when I knew that Matthias really had left for good.

***

Captain Cutlass's pirate treasure remained locked in the hall closet until Mom and Dad could figure out what to do with it. We were *so* rich, but Mom warned Alondra and me not to say a *word* about it to anyone. She and Dad were afraid that a burglar might break in and steal it.

One morning, I went downstairs and found Alondra, Dad, and Mom waiting for me in the kitchen. All the curtains were drawn. The pistols, swords, money, and jewels all lay on a big piece of canvas spread over the table.

I grinned and admired the glittering treasure. Even Alondra looked excited. "So...what's going on here?" I asked. I reached out one finger and traced the carving on one of the flintlock pistols. Alondra tried on a sparkly gold necklace that clinked as it moved.

"Dylan, don't touch that gun," Mom said. "It could be dangerous."

"Aw, Mom..."

"Well, did you find out how much it's worth?" Alondra asked. "The whole treasure, I mean?"

Mom and Dad looked at each other. They looked serious. *Too* serious. "Kids, your father and I have discussed this. We're not keeping the treasure."

"What? *Why?* We'd be *rich!*" I cried.

"You're *kidding* me!" Alondra wailed. "This is the best thing that's happened since we moved here, and now you're just getting rid of it? I don't believe this."

"We're going to donate it to the town museum," Dad said. "It rightfully belongs to the state of Maine. And it's a part of American history."

Before Dad packed everything up in the canvas, he let us each take a coin to keep for a souvenir. I wanted to take one of those old pirate pistols, or a sword, but Mom wouldn't even let me pick them up.

When we brought the treasure to the museum, Mrs. Cooper was so happy that she started to cry. "Do you know what this means, Roger?" she said in a quivering voice. "This lost treasure has been estimated to be worth over *twenty million dollars!* This is going to bring *prosperity* back to Salvation Point! You and your family might have just saved our town." She reached out to Dad, and hugged and kissed him. He looked embarrassed, but told her that it was the least he could do.

***

Dad painted our house and fixed it up so it looked exactly the way it did in that picture at the museum, when Matthias was still alive. He quit his job in Manhattan and went back to work at the boat shop, and Mom opened her own art gallery in town. Sometimes she and Alondra went back to the city if she had to go to an art reception or something, but she never made me go with them.

I liked my new school, even though it was so different from the one back in New York. There were only *ten* kids in the whole fifth grade! They didn't call me "the new kid;" instead, I was known as "the guy in the haunted house." I made some friends, although they were all too scared of my house to spend the night with me.

For a whole month, everyone in my class had to research and write a report about something – anything we wanted – in Maine. Of course, I wrote about our lighthouse. It was easy – I just had to remember everything that Matthias taught me. Mrs. Cooper even let me read his logbook. I wrote about what the lighthouse keepers' lives were like and how the lighthouse was built, how to light the lamp and trim the wicks, and how to wind the clockwork gears to make the Fresnel lens revolve. I got an A-plus! Mrs. Cooper was proud of me, and I think that Matthias would've been, too. I only wished that he were here to read it.

Even Alondra wasn't complaining as much. The lifeguard that she liked from the pool was in her class, and she made friends with some girls. They were all giggly and annoying, but they were nice, I guess. Alondra wasn't even as mean to me as she used to be. Neither was Mom. She cried when Dad finally told her that Matthias was the one who had brought me home. Then she made me sit down at the kitchen table the next day, and I thought I was in trouble, but she just told me that she was sorry for being so grumpy to me all summer. She apologized for saying that I was lying to her all the times that I had told her about Matthias. Then she hugged me, and promised me that from then on, she would try to understand me and listen to what I had to say. It was a start.

We had a long winter, with a lot more snow than we had in the city. Dad bought us all cross-country skis for Christmas, and taught us how to use them on the trails in the nature preserve. It was almost as much fun as sailing.

Thunder was still locked in the shed, but Dad started teaching me how to fix her up. I helped him with it every weekend, and soon she looked even *better* than new. Then one day, Dad took me to the boat shop to see what he did there.

"So, you're the boy who loves boats," Dad's boss said, as he shook my hand. "Your dad told me what a good job you did fixing up your little dinghy. In a few years, when you're old enough, I'll give you a job with us here."

"I'd like that," I said with a big grin. "I would *really* like that!"

Now that I had a *job* waiting for me, Mom and Dad would *have* to let me stay here to live! I didn't have to wait the whole year to find out. The next May – on the day I turned eleven – Dad took me to a big farm out in the country.

"This is a pet sanctuary," Dad said. "An animal rescue. Your mother and I have already filled out the paperwork, and we've been approved to adopt a dog. You can take your pick if you want…but there's a certain dog here that I want you to meet. I know that you've been wishing for him for a long time."

Dad took me in an office and talked to a smiling lady, who grabbed a leash and went into another room.

"This is Orion," the lady said as she led a huge, black dog out to meet us. "He needs a good home. I'm sure that he'll be glad to have a little boy to play with."

I was so happy, that I didn't even mind that she called me a *little* boy. Orion was my *Newfoundland*, just as big and fluffy as the ones in my dog book! He looked like a *bear!* When Quint and Sleeter get out of jail, they won't *dare* to bother me now.

"Dad?" I said, as we loaded Orion into the backseat. "Mom said that we couldn't have a dog at our apartment. Does this mean that…we're *staying?*"

"You got it," Dad said with a big smile. "Your mother didn't need a year to decide. She's grown to love it here as much as we do. You did really well in school here this year, and even Alondra's…starting to change her mind."

It was the best birthday *ever.*

***

Salvation Point was changing, but it was better than it was before. Since Captain Cutlass's legendary treasure had been found - or rather, had been discovered - tourists had started coming back to town. There was a TV special about the treasure, and articles in every newspaper in the country. One reporter interviewed my family and me, and took our picture in front of the lighthouse. A photographer for *National Geographic* magazine came and took pictures of the lighthouse, the treasure, and the rocks where Dad had found it. Even famous scientists had been coming to town to study it. The parking lot at the hotel was always packed. The ice cream shop opened again, and they talked about reopening the movie theater, too. People even started buying the abandoned houses and fixing them up. Dad said that the town was returning to the way that he remembered it when he was growing up here.

Sleeter was still in jail, but sometimes I saw Quint walking around town. If he spotted me, he always put his head down and hurried off in the other direction. Maybe he was scared of Orion. Or…maybe he thought that Matthias was still with me.

Matthias was the best friend that I had ever had, even though he was a grown-up…and a ghost. But I never saw him again. I missed him. I wished that I could still talk to him, and watch him work with the invisible old-time equipment in the lighthouse. But I hoped that he was happy now. I always wondered if he had found his family again...and if he ever thought about me.

Deep in my dresser drawer was the old lighthouse keeper's button and Indian head penny that Matthias had gotten back for me. I knew that I would never forget him.

And outside, the lighthouse beam continued to flash into my window and light up the night, the way I knew it always would.

About the Author

Jodi Auborn became interested in lighthouses and the ocean when she was fifteen years old and went on her first vacation to Cape Cod, Massachusetts. Later in life, she made several trips to Monhegan Island and other small towns in coastal Maine, all of which inspired the setting for the fictional town of Salvation Point.

She is the author of *Stormwind of the North Country* and *Secrets of the North Country*, teen novels set in New York State's Adirondack Mountains. She has also written a memoir titled *My Ten-Acre Wilderness.*

The author lives in Ticonderoga, NY. Learn more at www.jodilauborn.webs.com.

Made in the USA
Coppell, TX
21 November 2022

86790094R00115